STRAYS

Like

US

.

RICHARD

PECK

Dial Books *New York*

Published by Dial Books
A member of Penguin Putnam Inc.
375 Hudson Street
New York, New York 10014

Designed by Julie Rauer
Printed in the U.S.A. on acid-free paper
First Edition
1 3 5 7 9 10 8 6 4 2

Library of Congress Cataloging in Publication Data
Peck, Richard, date.
Strays like us/Richard Peck.
p. cm.
Summary: When her drug-addict mother can no longer
care for her, twelve-year-old Molly comes to stay with her
great-aunt, and slowly begins to realize that
others in the small town also feel as if they don't belong.
ISBN 0-8037-2291-5
[1. Social isolation—Fiction. 2. Interpersonal relations—Fiction.
3. Great-aunts—Fiction.] I. Title.
PZ7.P338St 1998 [Fic]—dc21 97-18575 CIP AC

To Amy Meriweather
and John Cardoza

Chapter

1
.
.
.

I'd lived in this town for twelve days, and I was up in a tree. The fork of a tree seemed the place to be, as cool as anywhere, and private.

But today a boy was up in another tree over there on the other side of the fence. It was leafy August, so he thought he could see me and I wouldn't know he was there. Boys think they can see you and you can't see them back. Boys think they do all the looking. But he got tired of me not noticing him.

"Want to hear a song?" he said in this high, reedy voice. I was supposed to be so surprised to hear a tree talk that I'd fall off my perch. "I know most of 'Achy, Breaky Heart.' Want to hear it?"

No. But I didn't say anything.

"I know some jokes," he said. "Want to hear one?"

No. Really no.

"Fella goes into a bar one day . . ."

He tapered off because he wasn't getting any encouragement from me. I wasn't up here to talk tree-to-tree with anybody.

1

"They say your name's Molly."

They were right, but it was my business.

"You got dropped off here. I don't know who by."

It was a social worker who brought me. It was just temporary. A temporary arrangement.

"They say your mama's not doing too good."

My mother had to go into a hospital until she was better. Then she'd come for me and take me away. That was the way it was going to happen. Why even mention it?

"I got dropped off too," he said in a softer voice. "My daddy's a traveling man. I been traveling with him, but now I can't. He was going to get me a dirt bike, but that's on hold right now. My mama died having me. My mama's the one who died. Mama's people wanted to raise me, but my dad said no way."

The big thunderheads drifted high over the trees. It looked cool up there, like August wouldn't last forever. I wanted time to pass, but I didn't want August over. You know how it is, not wanting summer to be over.

"I'll be in junior high here in a couple of weeks," he said.

We'd both been dropped off in this town, and we'd both be going into junior high. Too bad he was a boy. I could use a friend.

"You been dumped on your aunt Fay Moberly," he said.

She was my great-aunt, but I let that pass.

"Your aunt Fay hauls herself all over town in her ancient Dodge Dart. You can't keep a secret from her."

You probably couldn't. She was a practical nurse, which meant she had enough nurse's training to take care of people in their homes. So I supposed she knew everything about everybody. Most of her patients were old, and Aunt Fay was no spring chicken herself.

"Everything's old here," the boy said, picking up my thought. "These trees too. You better not eat these apples."

A hard little green apple hung in front of my face. I snapped it off its stem and took a big bite. It was no good, but it was crisp. He heard me chomp into it. I spit it out and held that part in one hand, the rest of the apple in the other, while he listened. It was so quiet you could hear bees.

I'd given up on him when he spoke again, real quiet now. "I won't know me a soul in junior high. Everybody will know everybody else. They're from here."

I wouldn't know a soul either. This had happened to me before, so I knew how bad it could be. That's why I wanted my mother to come back and get me before school started. That's why I was up this tree. I was counting off the days and trying to make each one of them long enough to bring my mother back.

The screen door of his house flew open, and his grandma came out on the back porch. She was so old-fashioned that she'd fling a pan of used water out in the yard. She flung it on bald ground because she didn't have any flowers to water. You could see where there used to be gardens in her backyard and Aunt Fay's too.

"Hooey, Willis Eugene!" she hollered out. She was a big old lady, big as Aunt Fay, with a hairnet on and a nightgown billowing around her. "Get in here for your dinner, and I'm talking about right now." It was high noon, but people called it dinner here. She went back inside, and the screen door banged behind her.

He'd have to drop down now and go up to the house, and he wasn't ready for me to see him yet. Some leaves shook. Then he fell like an apple out of his tree.

Though he wanted to drop down like a jungle fighter, he fell over sideways when he hit dirt. He jumped up real quick and went on up to the house, too proud to run. He could feel my eyes boring into his skinny back.

In the last week before school I slept late. It was one of my ways of holding back time. A lot of places where I'd lived with my mother, they made you get up and leave before seven o'clock.

On one of the mornings, I smelled coffee and heard voices behind the kitchen door. Aunt Fay went off to work at all kinds of times. This morning she was in her kitchen talking to somebody—I never knew who.

People came and went in her kitchen. Most of them wanted medical advice because she was cheaper than a doctor's appointment. I stopped this side of the kitchen door.

"They call it a hospital," Aunt Fay was saying. "I don't know."

She was talking about my mother, about Debbie. Aunt Fay didn't say her name, but I knew. I was here because my mother had to be put away, but only till she got better.

"Well, it's rough on you," the other voice said, an old down-home Missouri voice the way people talk here. "And there's another case like it right next door."

"The McKinneys?" Aunt Fay said. "Oh, you mean they've got Fred's boy back."

"Rough on them," the other voice said.

"If we don't take them in," Aunt Fay said, "where they going to go?"

"Well, I guess it's just temporary."

"Some things is more temporary than others," Aunt Fay said. I walked backwards down the hall until I couldn't hear any more.

The next morning Aunt Fay drove me to Marshalls in her Dodge Dart for my school clothes.

I didn't know what to get, but some girls milled around the mirror in the Back-to-School department. They were piling up tops and sweatshirts and jeans.

They were checking out skirts too, real short, and scoop-necked tops. But I couldn't see myself in those. They showed too much, and I didn't have enough.

None of it looked like school clothes to Aunt Fay, but she let me pick some things. I didn't try on anything because of the other girls in the dressing room. Then we went over to School Supplies.

"Was you in school at all last year?" Aunt Fay asked.

"I was in three or four," I said.

When we came to the notebooks and paper and erasers in shapes, I didn't know what kind to get, and neither did she, and there was nobody here buying anything. So I picked the first notebook I saw, and we left.

After we got home, I said, "What about my hair?" I raked a hand over it like I didn't care, but Aunt Fay saw through that. She dragged the kitchen stool out on the back porch and gave me a trim. It was like being in a barber shop with Aunt Fay looming over me and snipping around my ears with the kitchen scissors.

I was shaggy because my mother had always cut my hair. It was the one thing she was good at—cutting hair. She could do her own, reaching around behind and evening it up. Most of the time her hands were all over the place, but when they were steady, she could have worked in a beauty parlor.

"Well, I guess that looks all right." Aunt Fay stepped back to see. "Go inside and look in the mirror." But I didn't. I guess I thought if I couldn't see me, nobody else could either.

I moped to slow down the days. The town was still a mystery to me, even before I knew how many secrets it kept. I didn't want to know this town too well, because that meant I'd be staying. But I walked the way to school to see how long it took to get there. I did that two or three times.

Now it was the night before school, and I was up in Arlette's room under the eaves. Arlette was somebody Aunt Fay had rented the room to for a few months way back when. Forever after that, it was always called Arlette's room. Some of her bobby pins were still in the dresser drawers, and hangers hung at the back of the closet from her time. It wasn't really my room. Aunt Fay's bedroom was downstairs, though she slept some on the living-room couch in front of the TV.

Arlette's room was just the far end of the attic, walled in, with a window out over the slanting back-porch roof. But I'd never had a room to myself. I pretended it was my apartment in some city. I imagined a kitchenette along one wall and a bathroom without having to go downstairs.

I was on the bed, and my school clothes were hanging where I could see them. Had I been wearing a blindfold when I picked them? I didn't know which to wear on the first day or what went with what. I didn't care about clothes, but I didn't want to stand out. I'd as soon wear my Six Flags T-shirt and the raggedy shorts I'd lived in all summer. But a voice inside me said I better not. I was twelve, so I was beginning to hear little voices inside me.

I couldn't decide, and I wouldn't get undressed and go to sleep, because then the next thing you knew, it'd be morning.

It was still summertime. Why do you have to go back to school when it's still summertime? Nothing stirred. It was quiet as a tomb, until I heard the drainpipe rattle. My heart stopped to listen. The leaves on the passionflower vine rustled as somebody grabbed hold and started climbing.

If I'd had good sense, I'd have been down the stairs and all over Aunt Fay. But maybe I thought that if I didn't move, nothing else would happen.

Somebody was climbing the drainpipe. A shoe skidded. Then a ghost seemed to grunt as somebody pulled up onto the porch roof. The brittle old shingles crinkled, so now somebody was up there, crouching.

I could move an arm. I reached over and shut off my bedside lamp, like I'd be safer in the dark. I thought it might be all right to move my eyes but not my head. The window was screened because the bugs were terrible around here. I listened to a knee thump the shingles. Somebody was crawling up the slant of the roof toward my window. I wasn't doing a thing now. My brain was frozen in my skull. Though I never cried no matter what, a tear came out of my eye and ran down into my ear.

A shadow fell over the room. The screen wire sighed when a hand ran over it. Then a voice.

"Molly?" A hoarse whisper.

I sat straight up in the bed. Where did I get the notion that somebody who knew my name wouldn't kill me?

"Molly? It's Will. Will McKinney from next door?"

I wanted to wring his scrawny neck. What business did he have hanging on to my windowsill like a bat? We hadn't had a word to say to each other since that day in the trees, and I hadn't said anything then.

"Why don't you flip on your light and let me in?"

A terrible need to be cool came over me, and I dug the tear out of my ear.

"Come on," he said, real quiet. "Unhook the screen before I roll off."

"Roll off," I said.

"Aw, Molly," he said.

I flipped on the lamp. In the light his face was pale as a spirit with the night behind him, and his nose was flat against the screen. That was a sight in itself. I took my sweet time swinging my legs off the bed. It was just a step or two to the window, but I made it last.

"What do you think you're doing, anyway?"

"Let me in and I'll say."

When I scooted up the screen, he ducked under and dropped into the room. He was always dropping down out of someplace. This time he lit light. "I better be quiet." He pointed at the floor and meant Aunt Fay.

"You better get out of here," I said, whispering. "She'll skin me alive if she finds out I'm letting boys in off the roof." But you could hear her sleeping from here.

I hadn't seen Will up close. He wasn't as tall as I was. He was thin armed and knobby kneed, and his summer haircut was grown out. In June it must have been a buzz cut. Now it was down in his eyes. He had some freckles and a smudge on his nose from the screen. I didn't know what was keeping his shorts up.

Now he was standing there like it was my turn.

"You can sit on the bed a minute," I said, because there wasn't a chair. He plopped down, bouncing to try out the mattress. He looked around the room through the hair in his eyes, but there wasn't much to see, and he wasn't interested in my school clothes. His sneakered feet barely met the floor, but he worked his hands together like an old man.

"Well, here's the way it used to be," he said. "They used to have eight grades of grade school, then four years at the high school. Then they did away with that system. They built a new grade school up through sixth grade. It looks like a brooder house, out on South Main? Now they've put the junior high in the old grade-school building."

"So what?"

"I'm just putting you in the picture." He was still working his hands together. Looked to me like he was trying to put himself in the picture. "Anyway, that's where we'll be going tomorrow."

I didn't say anything. I just stood there with my hands sliding off my hips. I didn't really have hips.

"I'm enrolled," he said. "You enrolled?"

I shrugged. "I wasn't figuring on being here."

"Where'd you figure on being?"

I shrugged again.

"I knew I'd be here," he said.

He looked worried, and I'd seen some worried kids. He looked as worried as I felt. I glanced around at my clothes, hanging up like flat scarecrows. I hadn't taken the tags off because that felt too final. Then I read Will McKinney's mind, clear as a bell.

He was wishing I was a boy. I knew because I was wishing he was a girl. I didn't even like girls much, and they weren't that crazy about me, but I wished he was one.

With a girl I could say, What am I supposed to wear tomorrow? A girl could have come in the front door. A girl wouldn't be coming in off the roof. Oh, I might. But no other girl would.

"Here's what I was thinking," Will said. "You want to walk to school together tomorrow? You know, just the first day. That way both of us would know two people."

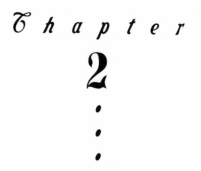

Chapter 2:
:
:

*T*hen the summer sun was pouring in the window like it didn't know what this day meant. The whole house smelled like a truck stop.

Down in the kitchen Aunt Fay was frying a pan of bacon and eggs. They were the first I'd seen here. Most days she'd be gone before I got up. Sometimes she stayed home and cooked all morning, making casseroles to freeze. I could have whatever I wanted out of the refrigerator, but we hadn't sat down to a meal together. Sometimes she didn't come in till nine at night, later even. She wasn't used to having anybody around to answer to.

She forked the bacon onto paper towels and turned off the gas. She was giving me a good send-off on my first day. I got my own juice out of the refrigerator, which she called the icebox.

Sliding the plate across the table, she settled in the other chair. Now for the first time we were face-to-face. She sat whenever she could, and she crossed her legs like a man, with the ankle of one on the knee of the other. On the ankle that didn't swell she wore a gold ankle bracelet. There was the cuff of her white pants and the big shape of her white shoe and in between a gold ankle bracelet. It fascinated me, like she might have tattoos. The wide neck of her white blouse showed the rings in her neck.

I forked into the egg, and she pointed at an envelope on the table. "It's a copy of your birth certificate. They may want to see that at school. The social worker brought it. Debbie give it to her. Your mother did."

So then I knew my mother never had planned to come back for me before school started. Maybe it was only in my mind that she'd said she would. Maybe I made that up. "You know anybody at that school?" I said to keep my eyes from filling up. They did that sometimes before I could stop them.

"Teachers? I wouldn't know them. That school you're going to used to be the grade school. All my grade-school teachers are out in the cemetery, pushing up daisies."

"Did you go to high school?" I wasn't sure.

"Some," she said. "I went to more high school than what Wilma McKinney did." Aunt Fay nodded to next door, to Will's grandma's house. "And I went oftener."

Somehow I'd cleaned my plate. "That was a good breakfast," I said, still visiting, still being polite.

Aunt Fay shrugged. "Oh well, I like to cook. Used to be I had the best eating out of my garden you ever tasted. Squash, even. But I don't have the time to mess with a garden now. I never was one for flowers. They put me in mind of the sickroom."

From here you could look up the hall through the house, if the kitchen door was open. Aunt Fay and I both saw Will out on the porch, just the slump of his shoulders and his flyaway hair. He was sitting on the top porch step like a potted plant, waiting for me. I slipped my birth certificate into my notebook and slid out of the chair.

"Here, don't forget your lunch." Aunt Fay handed me a brown bag. Then, as I started away, she said, "Hold it and bend over." She heaved herself up and took the pair of long scissors out of the knife drawer. "You missed a tag."

My jeans crinkled like roof shingles. Then somehow she was whispering in my ear. "Be careful of the McKinney kid."

"Why?" I whispered.

"Don't ask him about his dad."

"How come?"

"They say he's in jail."

Then Will McKinney and I headed off to junior high. I can see us yet, ambling along in the hotting-up day, like a pair of lost dogs along the side of the road.

The roots of old trees had pushed the sidewalk slabs out of line, so we walked uphill and down along the flat street. We trudged like we were walking the last mile, and Will didn't speak till we were waiting at the sign to cross Jefferson Street. "Watch yourself here. A lot of these cars have high-school people in them."

He was walking a little taller now. He'd puffed himself up, especially through the shoulders, trying to be bigger. Crossing Jefferson, he walked stiff legged. It didn't make him look older. It made him look like a windup doll, which is funny now but wasn't then. I caught a glimmer of what boys put themselves through.

We'd both practiced the route, so we knew the way, making the turn at the 7-Eleven in silence. Big yellow school buses gunned past us. We were in sight of the school when the dam broke and words burst out of him.

"What I wish is a UFO would set down right here in the street between us and school. You know how they do. They put down a ramp from their space capsule or whatever. The extraterrestrials come off it—Pod People or whoever. They could take us away, knock us out, give us examinations. Then bring us back after school."

I thought about it. "Looks to me like we're the Pod People," I said. "We're the ones from outer space."

Now the school rose up. Back by the parking lot was a new structure that turned out to be the gym and cafeteria, now that this was a junior high. But the main building was old as time. I could picture Aunt Fay going to grade school here.

Then Will cut out. I figured he would, but I couldn't believe how fast.

The front steps was a mob of strangers. Inside, it sounded like any school, that roar that pounds your head unless you're yelling too. I thought I'd have to report to the office and wondered where it was. But a woman was in the hall, trying to outyell the rest.

"Students from the grade school report to the gym. Students new to the system report to the auditorium."

The auditorium looked like classrooms put together, and up on the stage were cafeteria tables. In a row on the side the girls had staked out, two girls were sitting together. One threw out her hand to keep me from sitting next to her, so I sat a seat over. It took me a minute to notice that students new to the system filled up half the auditorium. At twelve you always think you're the only one.

They sure weren't from around here. You saw everything—black lipstick, nose rings, bare middles. And a lot of people were too jumpy to sit down. There were ten or twelve just on our side. Across the aisle half the boys were sitting up on their chair backs, and you had everything over there too—a lot of low-crotch denim and novelty haircuts and words written on their hands. But it was quieter in here, more of a dull roar, and you could smell the worry.

Somebody tramped on my feet and pushed past my knees. I looked up and it was Will. The girl put out her hand to keep him from sitting down but grabbed it back when he didn't notice. Settling in beside me, he said, "I might as well sit anywhere. Nobody knows anybody, except for these two over here on my other side. You suppose everybody's been dropped off?"

I couldn't believe it. "Couldn't some of them have moved here with their parents?"

"Do they look it?"

"No," I said. "They look like Pod People."

"Well then, it don't matter. Hey, we could even hold hands if we wanted to. Want to?"

"No, and neither do you, so quit trying to act older." But I didn't mind him being there.

There was no welcoming speech. It wasn't that kind of town. Here, people already knew everybody they wanted to. A teacher got up on the stage and told us to line up and bring whatever records we had.

I inched along with the rest, behind Will, watching how his ears splayed out. They still do, but back then his neck was skinnier. Skinny McKinney, but I didn't say so.

"I thought you were already enrolled," I said.

"I am, but they wanted a look at my credentials." He held up a transcript, so he'd been in some school long enough to have one. He wiggled it in the air so I couldn't see the grades. "California," he said. "I been all over." When we were stumbling up the steps to the stage, I dug for my birth certificate.

"That's a beginning," the man said when it was my turn. He had on a ball cap and a sweatshirt, with a whistle around his neck, so he must have been the coach. I didn't know. That school would never again be as big as it was on the first day.

I gave him my address when he asked, Cedar Street.

"Are you living with grandparents?" I didn't want to be stared at, but he hardly looked up.

"A great-aunt, Mrs. Fay Moberly." So that was a blank he could fill in on his form.

"And you're a Moberly too."

Yes, but we weren't blood kin, as people say around here. She married a man named Moberly whose brother was Debbie's dad. So Debbie was a Moberly because her father was. And I was a Moberly because I never had a father. I hoped the coach wouldn't ask.

"Were you in sixth grade last year?"

"Yes." More or less.

"Then you're in seventh now." He pushed across a class schedule, and my hand shook when I took it. But he was looking past me, snapping his fingers and saying, "Next."

There were more of us extras than they'd bargained for, so they ran out of desks. They had to drag in straight chairs and line them up across the backs of the classrooms. That's where I wanted to sit, all day long in every class—on a chair at the back, just visiting.

Still, you could see how things worked here, even

from the back row. We were mixed in with those who'd come from the grade school. The girls in their scoop-necks and skirts, the boys' shirts that were a little bit country, a little bit cowboy. Everybody matched and blended in with everybody else, and nobody sat by newcomers. They were dressed up for the first day, but I didn't know that.

The cafeteria was a room past the far end of the new gym. It reminded me of the places Debbie and I went to eat free—all those long tables of people eating too fast, or too slow because they were trying to stay indoors. It was noisier here, of course.

I was at the end of a girls' table when Will turned up. He pulled a chair next to me. When I opened my lunch, it was half a tuna sandwich and half Velveeta cheese with bacon. An apple, a box of milk.

When Will got into his sack, he came up with the same lunch exactly. It looked like the other half of my tuna sandwich, the other half of the Velveeta. Everything the same. I stared, and he noticed too. I was about to ask him why, but he looked off over the lunchroom and said, "I wonder if they let you shoot hoops in the gym after school."

We got through the day, and the only thing I learned was that I was so far behind in math, I never would catch up. I could read and write—I'd picked that up along the way. Then after school Will fell into step with me on the way home. It was such an old-time town that the side streets were still brick. It was summer again as we walked past porches screened green with vines. The houses were plain and alike, and I guessed this was the poor side of town, but I'd seen poorer.

"You ever live in a house before?" Will asked, pushing into my thoughts.

To keep him from asking more, I said, "No. And I never had a room of my own until I had Arlette's."

"I wish I did," he mumbled.

"Wish what?"

"Wish I had a room to myself." Then he peeled off for his house.

His grandma never seemed to leave the place, and Aunt Fay was rarely home in the afternoon. I went on, not wondering why Will and I had the same lunch or why he didn't have a room to himself. I flopped down on the top porch step where he'd waited for me that morning. My notebook was on my knees, and the afternoon shadows were beginning to reach across the old brick street.

Every house had a front porch, though some were glassed in for an extra room. Nobody sat out on them. Somebody, maybe Aunt Fay herself, had once painted her porch ceiling robin's-egg blue, but it was flaking. There were still two hooks where a porch swing had hung. I wondered if she used to sit out and talk across to Mrs. McKinney, before they got too old and too busy.

I'd made it through the first day of school, and it hadn't been as bad as dreading it. So I had a little talk with my mother, just in my mind. Now it was too late for her to come for me before school started. But Debbie, I told her, come when you can.

Chapter

3
.
.
.

I hung on the edges of school and watched, learning the names of people who didn't know mine. Even the teachers seemed slower to know us out-of-towners, and I thought they were eyeing us for signs of trouble. I saw signs they didn't.

Somebody wrote on a stall door in the girls' rest room:

> I'M HERE AND NOT HERE
>
> WILL I BE HERE NEXT YEAR?

I could have written it myself, except it was in black lipstick. But it was somebody like me.

I'd been in rougher schools, and bigger, and I was used to being on my own. I'd never made friends anywhere because I might come back to wherever we were living and find Debbie packing to go. She always wanted to move on to someplace she thought might be better or to follow somebody she liked. Her eyes would be bright that day, not glazed. "Bus station eyes," I called them. So I wouldn't be going back to that school, not even to clean out my desk. It wasn't worth making a friend I'd have to leave. I never got too near people, and I'd never let them get too near me, and that's the way it had always been.

If we came out of our doors at the same time, Will and I would walk to school together, sometimes on opposite sides of the street. He had a new shirt from Sears that was a little bit country, a little bit cowboy. He'd sit down at one corner of a boys' lunchroom table, but I didn't see anybody talking to him. After school he hung around to shoot hoops or whatever. They'd put together a junior-high football squad, but I figured he was too scrawny.

Then one day I got acquainted with Rocky Roberts. Real quick.

I didn't use the girls' rest room during the school day. With only three stalls and three sinks, there was a line to get in, and I didn't want to be late for class. I still thought no teacher knew me, and I was trying to keep it that way. I'd try to wait till after school.

The sinks were set close to the floor from when it was a grade school, but the toilets were full-size. I was in there one afternoon, trying to imagine Aunt Fay using one when she was in grade school. I suppose I saw her as she was now, gray hair and glasses, but small, with her pinafore hiked up and her legs swinging. I smelled smoke from the stall next door but didn't think much about it.

I was at the middle sink washing my hands when one of the stall doors opened behind me. Low in the mirror, I saw Rocky Roberts come swaggering out. I don't know what I thought. Maybe I wondered if I was in the wrong rest room. He was a boy. And he'd been smoking something in that stall. Two crimes.

He was short, but tough as a boot, with mean eyes. His little Levi's rode low to show the waistband on his underpants. The sleeves on his little black body shirt were rolled up over his shoulders. Zigzags were trimmed into the sides of his haircut. I didn't know if he was wearing gang colors from his last school. He was as far off his turf as I was.

I couldn't quite believe he was in the girls' rest room, but then he could be anywhere he wanted to be. Short as he was, he knew how to look dangerous. He'd put his head down in class and sleep, right through decimals or *Where the Red Fern Grows*, and the teachers let him.

Now he was standing behind me, and still I stood there, soaping my hands. I couldn't see him in the mirror. I could only see me. His hand snaked around, and I felt it grab my chest. He'd had to reach up. I still didn't believe this was happening, though I'd been to schools where I wouldn't have dared go into the rest room at all.

I whirled around and popped him one. I don't know which one of us was more surprised. Yes I do. He was. He had a nose full of knuckles before he knew it. His head snapped back, and his boot cleats scraped the floor as he keeled over backwards. I heard his head hit. Now he was scrabbling around like a crab. Why didn't I run? I looked down, and he was at my feet on all fours. His head sagged, and a drop of blood splattered on the white tile.

Did I think he was down for the count? Rocky? His fist came up from nowhere and connected with my chin. It was a glancing blow, or it would have jarred loose every tooth in my head. I bit my tongue, and it hurt so bad I went blind for a moment. His little hand, that hand that had grabbed me, reached for the sink. He was heaving himself up, and I didn't have a lot of time. I brought my knee up fast and caught him on the nose again. This was pure luck.

I thought I'd bitten off my tongue and would never speak again, and he was wheezing. Since I'd rearranged his nose, twice, he had the sense to duck out of my range. But he was on his feet, boots braced, bobbing and weaving. Then he lunged for my neck with both hands.

But my arms were longer. I went for him, slapping with both hands in a quick left-and-right to keep him from strangling me.

The rest-room door opened.

Miss Throckmorton had Rocky in one fist and me in the other, marching us across to the gym. I suppose her job was to check the rest rooms after school. Well,

Rocky was in the wrong one. But when Miss Throck-morton found us, I was winning the fight and I was bigger, so I didn't know where she stood.

Then we were in her office off the girls' locker room. She was the gym teacher and doubled as school nurse because she had a first-aid kit. "You there and you there," she said in her gym-class voice, separating us on chairs.

I opened my mouth to say something, who knows what, and blood trickled out of both sides and down my chin. Rocky's nose was running with blood, like a faucet. There was blood down both our fronts, and a smear of his on the knee of my jeans.

It was all over by then, the fighting part. Miss Throckmorton jammed some kind of padding into my mouth after she had a look at my teeth, wiping blood off them with her thumb. Then she was standing over by Rocky with one hand on the back of his neck, holding a wet cloth to his nose. I thought I'd have heard it crack if I'd broken it. She was back and forth between us, moving fast in her gym shorts.

I didn't know what was coming next. Right now there was nothing to do but look at my knuckles where the skin had been and watch Rocky. His arms dangled and his head was thrown back and his mouth hung open. He was limp as a rag while Miss Throck-morton worked on him.

Rocky was in shock. Nobody had ever turned on him before, not to mention a girl. You could see that.

Wherever he'd been, people had always gotten out of his way. Later in the year with longer to watch him, I might have gotten out of his way too, if I could.

I thought we'd both bleed to death. The padding in my mouth got bigger and bigger, and I was swallowing blood behind it. But I noticed something out of the corner of my eye. Somebody was standing in the door that opened onto the echoing gym. It was Will, with a basketball in the crook of his arm, watching.

Mr. Russell breezed in past him. He taught us social studies, and now I figured out he was the principal too. I should have known. He was the only man teacher who wore a jacket and tie, but I hadn't sorted out all these people. His eyes skimmed over Rocky and me. I wondered if he was the kind who faints at the sight of blood. Some men do. He went straight to the phone on Miss Throckmorton's desk and started making calls. I strained to hear but couldn't.

They let us cool our heels. It felt like a year. Rocky's eyes were beginning to dart everywhere but at me. He had sly eyes, and they glittered over the wet cloth on his nose. As he looked back and forth, I could see the lightning bolts carved into his hair. He was thinking about cutting and running, but it was too late for that. Something else happened, in the blink of an eye.

A woman charged into the office. She wore black leather pants and high-heeled shoes, and a vest that laced up the front, leaving her big arms bare. She had a huge head of stiff blond hair, frosted.

She saw Rocky and made right for him. In a blur the woman's big arm came out, and she slapped Rocky off the chair. Again I heard his head hit tile. I nearly swallowed my wadding. First me and now this woman. It wasn't Rocky's day. He started moaning, rolling back and forth on the floor and pulling up his knees.

Mr. Russell had whipped around and said a word I didn't catch. He was heading for this woman and nearly kicked Rocky in the head to get there. He danced around him, while in the background Miss Throckmorton stared.

"And that's for starters!" the woman yelled at Rocky, squatting down on her high heels and bending over him.

Mr. Russell didn't risk taking her by the arm. "Who *are* you?" he said in a wailing voice.

"I'm his grandmother," the woman roared, "and you called me away from my work!"

I wondered what her job was.

Mr. Russell looked lost. I'd figured everybody knew everybody else in this town, but he was looking at Rocky's grandmother as if he'd never seen anybody like her in his life.

"And when I get him home, I'll turn him every way but loose. I'll mop and wax the floor with the little—"

"Hey, Marlene, how you doing?"

We all looked at the door, and Rocky's grandmother pivoted around. It was Aunt Fay there, in her white pants and top with the keys to the Dodge Dart in her hand. She filled up the door. Another big woman. Miss Throckmorton stood motionless at her desk, still staring.

It took Rocky's grandmother a moment to put it together. Then she pointed at me, and I flinched. "Is that one yours, Fay?"

"You could say so," Aunt Fay said.

It looked like I'd been released into Aunt Fay's custody. Will was in the backseat. Maybe she'd told him to get in the car. Maybe he just hadn't wanted to miss anything. I'd spit out the wadding, fearing my tongue would come with it. Now I held the bloody mess of cotton in my hand, examining it for something to do. I'd already found out that drying blood turns brown. I'd learned that not long before.

Aunt Fay drove one handed with an elbow propped out the window. And I was hoping that when we got home, Debbie would be there. Debbie sitting out at the curb in a new car with somebody she liked, Debbie waiting to take me away.

Nobody spoke till we swung out of the school parking lot. I didn't think I wanted to hear whatever Aunt Fay was going to say. She took up more than her share of the front seat.

But Will spoke first, piping up from the back of the car. "That big leather woman was *mean*."

"Tell me about it," Aunt Fay said. "I went to school

with her. You should have seen her before she got civilized."

She'd gone to school with Aunt Fay? How could this be? "But she's a frosted blond," I said, "and wears high heels."

I felt Aunt Fay's glance. "Don't let her kid you. That hair come out of a bottle. She's my age. In fact she's a year older, because she had to repeat fifth grade. What happened?"

"He grabbed me," I mumbled, meaning Rocky. "He started it."

"I don't doubt it," Aunt Fay said. "Tough little customer, isn't he? Talking about tough, you should have seen his mother. Marlene Bledsoe's girl. They about got up a posse and run her out of town on a rail."

"Why?"

"Never mind. Where'd it happen?"

"In the girls' rest room," I said. "I was at the sink, and he came out of a stall and—"

"They still have those sinks low to the floor?"

I nodded.

"Me and Wilma McKinney got into it in there one time. Will's grandma, that is." Aunt Fay nodded back at him. "She could be sassy, and she said something I took exception to. I stuck her head under the tap and like to have drowned her. She had a big old bow in her hair, and it was sopping. She was so mad, she didn't speak to me for an hour."

I wondered if I was off the hook here. "Did the

3 0

school call you at work?" I said, thinking about Rocky's grandmother, Marlene.

"No." Aunt Fay's eyes were on the street. "I was over at Wilma McKinney's."

"You could hear your phone from there?"

"No. They called me there."

"How'd they know—"

"I told them," Will said from the backseat. "When I was shooting hoops, I saw Miss Throckmorton dragging you and Rocky across the gym to her office. I run up and told the principal. You were a mess."

We were down by the 7-Eleven now, waiting for a gap in the Jefferson Street traffic.

"Where'd he grab you?" Will said, and I guess he was trying to help.

"My top part," I mumbled. "My chest."

"That's harassment," Will said. "You've got a case there. That's definitely harassment."

"Is that what they call it?" Aunt Fay said. "Then Marlene really will mop and wax the floor with that kid. She's a cocktail waitress out at the Ramada."

So that's what her job was.

Aunt Fay made the turn in front of a Wagoneer. "Look," she said to me, "I've got a full load as it is, and a bad leg. I'm in and out. Maybe I've taken on more than I can handle here. Maybe I've bit off more than I can chew. You know I never had kids."

I wanted to tell her it was the first real fight of my life, but I couldn't prove it. From the backseat Will's voice welled up. "It was Rocky's fault. What was he doing in the girls'—"

"I got that part of it," Aunt Fay said. "All I'm saying is I can't be running to that school every whipstitch. There's limits on what I can do." She turned her head and looked back at Will, a long look. I just sat there, picking skin off my knuckles.

Then from the silence of the backseat, Will spoke again. "I'll keep an eye on her."

I could have popped him one, and Aunt Fay swallowed hard. I'd never heard her laugh, but she'd just come close.

"And throw that wad of cotton out the window," she said to me. "I'm sick of looking at it."

"That's littering," Will said, but in his smallest voice.

In some schools they kick you out for fighting, no matter what. In others, if they kicked everybody out for fighting, there'd be nobody left. And if I had a case for harassment or whatever, would I have to take Rocky Roberts to court? I'd seen Court TV, and I didn't like it. The next morning I went to school with my stomach in a knot and my tongue smarting. Last night Aunt Fay had dabbed disinfectant on it with a Q-Tip, saying, "There's not a whole lot you can do for a tongue."

Rocky wasn't even in school, but then he wasn't in school a lot. Besides, I'd made some alterations on his nose, and he might not want to show his face. So that left me. I supposed everybody knew. I supposed they were buzzing and looking at me the minute I turned my head. I looked back before yesterday when I'd been invisible, and it seemed like some other school. I lived through homeroom.

The first period was Mr. Russell's social studies. I moved from the back row to the middle, hoping the crowd would swallow me. Then he called on me by name. I remember why. He asked me if Haiti was an island, and the room waited to hear me say I didn't know. But I knew things from watching TV, if we were living in a motel and had a TV. I'd watch *Nightline*, waiting for Debbie to come home. "No," I said. "It's part of an island." So Mr. Russell knew me now and had spotted where I was sitting. He let me walk out after class, and the morning crept by. Every minute weighed a ton.

By noon I'd decided that nothing was going to happen. They were going to turn a blind eye on both of us, Rocky and me—two of a kind. As long as I didn't pop a local's nose, maybe I was home free.

I got to an empty lunch table as soon as I could. Then when the table filled, there was an empty seat beside me and another across from me and whispering at the other end. I smoothed the brown bag for a place mat under my lunch. I was trying to be civilized.

Will dropped down beside me. He'd bought his

lunch. It was pizza day, pizza and nachos and choco-late milk.

"Keeping an eye on me?" I muttered.

"Everybody is," he said. "Want a bite?" He held a pizza slice high to see how far the cheese would stretch.

Then who started across the room but Nelson Washburn. He was a tall blond kid, the tallest in seventh grade. Every girl at the table looked at him. They looked at him all day long. He leaned over me like I wasn't there. "McKinney," he said to Will, "are you a girl?"

I never looked up.

"Say what?" Will's voice hadn't changed, but Nelson's had.

"You heard me. What do you think you're doing at a girls' table? Do you know how that looks? Listen, you're new. I don't know where you're from, and I don't want to know. It doesn't bother me personally, but it's not the way we do it here, okay?"

I took a careful bite out of my sandwich, favoring my tongue, tending to my own business.

Then Will piped up as Will will. "Washburn, I thought you were coming over here to congratulate Molly Moberly."

"For what?" Nelson said, still not looking down at me, though I could have taken a bite out of his sleeve.

"For whipping Rocky Roberts's tail. Do you see

Rocky around school today? Peaceful, isn't it? Rocky's big old mean grandma's got him at home today, mopping and waxing the floor with him. You can thank Molly for that. Somebody had to do it, and here she sits." He nudged me. "It was a job that had to be done, and I don't picture you doing it. Old Rocky come up on you, and you'd be wondering if he had a boxcutter. Molly never even thought boxcutter."

That was true.

"Old Molly here whipped Rocky's tail, and Rocky could whip yours. She plastered his nose all over his face, and he could bring you down like a tree." Will jerked a small thumb at me. "This is one tough tootsie, and I'm keeping on her good side because I wouldn't want her for an enemy. That's why I'm at a girls' table, Washburn. Okay?"

My ears were in flames, and Nelson Washburn had to be surprised. You could talk back to teachers, but nobody talked back to him. He gazed far down at Will. Then he shook his head and walked away, stopping for a word at another table like he was just out for a stroll. He was about to be elected class president, so he campaigned a lot in the lunchroom anyway.

"'One tough tootsie'?" I muttered. "McKinney, somebody ought to lock up your mouth and throw away the key."

"And you can stop pretending you're not here,

Molly. You're here, and everybody knows it." Will kicked back and tied a knot in his chocolate-milk straw. "I'm in," he said.

"In what?"

"I'm just in. Till today Nelson Washburn acted like he didn't know my name. Now he's giving me the benefit of his advice."

I didn't know if that proved Will was in or not. But then these things might be easier for a boy.

"And you're in," he said. "You whipped Rocky Roberts's tail."

"You keep saying that. Somebody ought to—"

"It took a while, but we're both in, even strays like us. And there'll be more of us coming. You know, even some of these people who came from the grade school are like us. They just got here sooner. And we got here ahead of some who are on the way. The world's full of people coming back to old people in old towns like this one. It's like a trend. Get used to it."

"I don't get used to anything," I said, muttering low. "I don't care if I'm in or out. I probably won't be staying."

"Maybe you won't," he said. "Maybe you will."

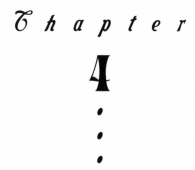

Chapter 4:

_A_fter lunch we had to go outside for language arts. They'd brought in a row of portable classrooms to handle the overflow, so the field south of the gym looked like a motel.

Ms. Lovett put things on the blackboard in her portable, and people didn't pay much attention. Today it was a very plain poem by Emily Dickinson.

> _Fame is a bee._
> _It has a song—_
> _It has a sting—_
> _Ah, too, it has a wing._

I could almost relate to it. Maybe I hadn't heard fame's song, but I'd felt its sting. And I hoped my fame would wing away, or I would.

Halfway through class my eyes bugged out of my head. Ms. Lovett kept a neat desk, a clean blotter with her attendance book centered on it, stacks of paper in straight piles. And at one end—my notebook.

This is how tense I'd been all day, and all night too. I'd lost my notebook and hadn't missed it. Yesterday I'd carried it into the rest room and put it down on the next sink while I washed my hands. Or did I carry it across to Miss Throckmorton's office? Whatever. But there it was on Ms. Lovett's desk. It was mine. There were spatters of brown blood on it.

We were filling in workbook blanks that day. When the bell rang, I thought about trying to snatch the notebook off the desk when she wasn't looking, but she was looking.

"I need my notebook," I said in a small, ghostly voice, making myself look at Ms. Lovett. Most adults were the same age to me, but she was young. And different, with big brown eyes in a fragile face. She almost always wore black.

"I looked inside," she said. "How did you learn to do that?"

She opened the cover to one of the pages, but it was all right because we were in the portable alone now. It was a picture I'd drawn across the ruled blue lines, a young woman's face. The curls of her hair, the tendrils, filled all four corners. Ms. Lovett turned the page.

It was the young woman on a sofa with her feet tucked under her. I'd worked and worked and erased and erased, and still I hadn't gotten the line of her back right. I'd drawn in a pillow to hide her back but erased it.

On the next page she was in bed asleep, and I'd worked hard to draw her arm hanging down and her knuckles just brushing the floor.

"You're very good," Ms. Lovett said.

"I can't draw hands," I said.

"But it's so clearly the same person. All these different studies. Who is she?"

"Just somebody I made up."

It was my mother, of course. It was Debbie. Not the real Debbie, but one I could carry around and keep with me. I'd done twenty pictures of her so far, and I had a lot of pages left. I thought by the time I'd filled up the whole notebook with Debbie, she'd be back for me. Sometimes I worked fast, hoping to hurry her. Sometimes I worked slow, to give her all the time she needed.

"You left it in the gym office. Miss Throckmorton brought it over to me. She said she didn't know anything about art but thought I might."

So there were these two teachers working behind my back, knowing who I was.

"I wish the school had an art teacher," Ms. Lovett said. "I think there used to be art teachers in the schools here."

"They probably can't afford them anymore," I said, firming my jaw, "now that so many of us got sent back here."

"I don't know," she said. "This is my first year."

39

So that was why she looked younger than a teacher. Maybe that was why she never smiled in class. "Can I have it back?" I asked her.

"Of course. Put your name in it."

"Why? It gets found anyway." I never put my name on my things because they came and went. This notebook was my most precious possession, and I hadn't put my name in it.

"Work as good as yours should be signed," she said.

At the door of the portable, I looked back to thank her since I was just visiting here. Then I cut out for math and spent that hour drawing petals around the blood splotches on my notebook cover and giving them stems and leaves to turn them into flowers, brown autumn flowers. Even though I wasn't the flower type.

Was it that afternoon when I came home and found Aunt Fay in the front hall, waiting for me? She was in her nurse's whites, and the car keys were jangling in her hand. She'd never been there when I got home from school. She was always someplace else, and I suppose I was a latchkey kid, except she never locked her house. "What would they steal? My TV's black and white," she told me once.

"I've taken on Mrs. Voorhees," she said. "You can give me a hand."

In the car she jumped the clutch, and we lurched

40

forward. "I haven't got time to take on another patient," she said, scattering the fallen leaves down Cedar Street before one of her quick swerves out onto Jefferson.

So I supposed she'd taken on Mrs. Voorhees because of me, because of another mouth to feed and my school clothes.

"I've worked for her before. Her and me go way back. She'll wear a person out."

"Mean?"

"I don't know about mean," Aunt Fay said, "but difficult. She's in a big house with nothing to think about but her aches and pains."

"What am I supposed to do?"

"Oh, I don't know." Aunt Fay waved me away. "Just play it by ear. She likes company. She don't know it, but she does. She likes attention."

I thought maybe Aunt Fay was taking me to work to keep an eye on me. Maybe I was the one who needed some attention.

We were downtown now, which was empty storefronts and cannons in the courthouse square. Then we charged along Lee Boulevard up the only hill. I hadn't been up here to see how the houses got nicer. I pictured old Mrs. Voorhees in a ruined castle with lightning rods.

Aunt Fay skidded onto Park Place, and here the houses were like mansions to me. She pulled up in front of one. It was a big rosy brick with white shutters. The only Halloweeny thing about it was how the shrubs grew up over the windows. The door opened before Aunt Fay could ring the bell.

"Well, Rose," she said to a woman in a nylon uniform.

"I'm just going to run on home and feed and water my kids," the woman said. "I'll be back directly to feed her." She pointed upstairs.

"How's her appetite?"

"She eats like a hired hand. I don't know where she puts it." Then Rose was gone, and we were in the front hall. It was kind of gloomy, but it reminded me of a house people live in on TV.

"What this place needs is a good airing." Aunt Fay started up the curving stairs. I kept with her, though this was about as far as I wanted to go.

She thumped a door and walked into a room as dim as downstairs. I knew there'd be somebody in a bed.

"Fay?" a voice said. "You been playing hard to get. I was beginning to think you'd retired and put your feet up."

"Well, here's how it is, Edith." Aunt Fay planted a hand on her hip. "I've got mirrors in my house. It wouldn't do to sit around watching myself starve to death."

A snort came from the bed that sounded like Aunt Fay herself, trying not to laugh.

"How are you?"

"I'm just as you see me," Mrs. Voorhees said. "I fell out of bed last night. Who's that with you?"

I'd kept behind Aunt Fay, but she waved me around. "This here's Molly."

I edged around her. I had to. A little woman sat propped up in bed. There was a reading light on, with a crooked shade, but she hadn't been reading. She just sat there in the bed with her hands arranged in front of her, and she gave me a quick, hard look. Then she blinked me away.

I chanced a glance to see her fingernails were bright, and so was her lipstick. She was made up like a doll.

"Are your medicines in the kitchen?" Aunt Fay asked her.

"For all the good they do," Mrs. Voorhees said.

"I'll just run down there and check them over, and I'm going to have to call your doctor."

"If you can get him," the old lady said. "He doesn't return my calls."

Then Aunt Fay was gone, and it was just me in the center of the room and the little old Barbie doll woman in the bed with her eyes trained on me. They seemed bigger than they really were. She'd drawn in large lashes over eye shadow. "You going to be a nurse when you grow up?" she said.

That was the last thing in this world I'd ever want to be. "I don't know yet," I mumbled.

"Just taking it a day at a time, are you?"

I nodded. That was exactly what I was doing.

"And speak up," she said, "so a person can hear you."

"I bit my tongue, so I talk funny."

"You *look* funny," she said. "Do you own a dress?"

I shook my head. I didn't think even Aunt Fay owned a dress. "Just jeans for school and shorts for summer."

"At your age I wouldn't walk out of the house without wearing a dress. And petticoats. I bet you don't know what a petticoat is."

"Some kind of coat?"

"It's a half-slip, real frilly with lace." Old Mrs. Voorhees stroked the little jacket she was wearing over her nightgown. It was satin with lace around the collar and cuffs. I'd never seen anything like it. "I'd haul off and wear two or three petticoats to make my skirt twirl. You better make yourself useful." She had a strange ringing voice. "Tuck in my sheets. My feet feel a draft. Do you know how to do hospital corners?"

"What are they?"

"If you don't know what they are, then you don't know how to do them. You can pull up a chair and sit over here by the bed."

Then I knew she couldn't really see me. I was just a blur. Even when I pulled up the chair, she had to squint. She needed her glasses but wouldn't wear them. Too vain. Right from the start I seemed to know things about her and how her mind worked.

"I know what you're thinking," she said. "I can read your mind. You're wondering what I was like as a girl, wearing all my petticoats."

"That's right."

"So many men in this town wanted to marry me that I told them they'd just have to take their turn and I'd get around to them all."

I must have stared. "How many did you marry?"

"It was just a joke," she said. "Three."

Still, I stared, I guess.

"Can you do manicures?" Her hand came out, and it was like a little paw, with spots and blue veins and these long, red nails. A ring hung loose on one finger, and the diamond in it looked like the headlight off a car.

"I chip off the paint," she said. "What else do I have to do? Reach in that drawer and get out the polish remover and that Jungle Red."

So I gave her a manicure, my first.

"Do you know what cuticles are?" she said. "Be real careful with mine."

I rubbed away on the old polish with Kleenex and the remover, and I knew I better get every speck. The polish wasn't that chipped. She wanted somebody to hold her hand. Her fingers were brittle as old paper. I missed some places with the Jungle Red and had to go back, but she was more or less patient.

When Aunt Fay finally came back, she found me bending over Mrs. Voorhees's hands, giving her a manicure, the two of us in the circle of light from the crooked shade. Aunt Fay stood in the door, watching the two of us there together.

"Ever see anybody so prissy?" she said in the car on the way home.

"Behind the makeup, is she real old?"

"Edith?" Aunt Fay said. "She's not old. She's my age. Her and Marlene Bledsoe and Wilma McKinney and me were in the same class."

"Oh," I said. "Was she pretty back then?"

Aunt Fay lifted her big shoulders. "Pretty is as pretty does. I'll tell you one thing. She was boy crazy."

"She married three," I said.

"At least," Aunt Fay said.

"Is she rich?"

"She's feathered her nest right well for somebody who never done a day's work in her life. The money come from Voorhees. He was old when she married him, and he left her pretty well fixed. The house alone would be worth something, if it was in a better town."

Now Aunt Fay was aiming the Dart at the garage. "I'm going to look in on Wilma McKinney," she said. "You skin up to the house. Later on I'll rustle us up some supper."

So I went on in the house and gave myself a manicure, my first—without the Jungle Red.

I'd never been next door to the McKinneys' place, and I'd hardly set eyes on Will's grandma since that first day in the tree. I pictured her living her whole life in that nightgown. And I didn't even know if Aunt Fay liked Mrs. McKinney or not. You couldn't really know that kind of thing about Aunt Fay. I didn't know if she liked me.

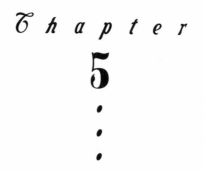

Chapter 5

Halloween came and went, and the leaves were falling fast. Will ate lunch up nearer Nelson Washburn's table now, and something happened to me that looked like a miracle. I met Tracy Pringle. It was one of those miracles that only last a moment.

To keep from coming straight home every afternoon, I'd found the public library. It was almost downtown, a little old stone building with CARNEGIE carved over the door. I holed up in the reading room there because I didn't have a desk in Arlette's room, and I'd taken to doing homework. I thought maybe I could teach myself some math, and I wanted a good social studies grade to show Mr. Russell I was civilized. And I liked doing language arts for Ms. Lovett. Who knew what kind of school I'd be in next? I kept my notebook handy.

Then one day at the library a voice spoke over my shoulder. "Are those drops of blood?"

I looked up, and she was like a girl in a Back-to-School catalogue. Her wool skirt was plaid, and she wore a sweater with buttons over a snow-white blouse. The barrettes in her hair were a little bit grade school, but she seemed older than I was. I looked away to keep from being blinded because she was so perfect. "They used to be blood drops, but now they're flowers."

"I've seen you in here before." She settled on the edge of the chair beside me and perched there. "Sometimes I'm just leaving when you get here."

But why? I came here right from school.

"I've been looking things up about the Internet," she said. "I'm getting a computer. Do you have one?"

I shook my head. I hadn't even seen a computer at school. "Are you in eighth grade?"

"I'll be fourteen Friday," she said. "Should I have a party and invite you?" She spoke as if she'd just thought of it, in a rush like she didn't have much time.

"Sure," I said, though she couldn't mean it. I didn't know how to talk to a girl like this. Will would. He'd think of something.

"My name is Tracy Pringle," she said. "I don't go to school."

There were times I hadn't either, but . . .

"I'm home schooled."

"What does that mean?"

"My mother teaches me, at home. So many bad things happen at schools." Her eyes traced the blood spots on my notebook cover. "I'd better be going now. My mother will be by to pick me up."

49

"Do you live way out in the country?"

"No, just up the hill." She meant the hill where people like Mrs. Voorhees lived in big houses. "See you tomorrow?"

I nodded, not wanting to sound eager. "My name's Molly Moberly."

"I know. It's on your notebook."

Then she was gone, and I sat there in the shadowy reading room, wondering if I'd dreamed her.

All my memories of that week are of meeting Tracy after school. I'd make a run for the library, throat tight for fear I'd miss her. She was always there, though she never stayed long. Every day she wore a different outfit. I pictured her laying out everything the night before, matching everything. Her sneakers were the cleanest I'd seen.

At the library we sat side by side, elbows touching. Her handwriting was small, like an adult's, and she outlined the notes she took on the computer manuals. She used different colors to highlight. Her pages were like rainbows.

You could talk in the reading room. We were usually the only ones there, but Tracy didn't think we should. It gave us a chance to write notes, like the girls in class.

Do you like school?

one of her notes asked.

I wrote back,

So-so. Ms. Lovett's nice.
Do you like home school?

She drew a smiley face for an answer. Her notes were from a tiny notepad with pink pages. I wrote on scraps. On Wednesday she wrote,

Do you know any boys?

I wrote back,

one

She wrote,

Is it Nelson Washburn?

That made me laugh because I didn't know how to giggle. "He's a neighbor of ours," she said in a small, breathy voice like Ms. Lovett's, without waiting to write it out. "I know him, but he doesn't know me."
I wrote,

I know him too, sort of.
I guess I know two boys.

I left out Rocky Roberts.

On Thursday she wrote,

why don't you ever take notes in your notebook?

I just smiled. Some girls would have reached over and grabbed it, but Tracy wouldn't.

Just as she was leaving, I slid a scrap of paper across to her. She hadn't noticed how I'd been sneaking peeks at her. I'd drawn a quick sketch of her, how her hair fell, framing her profile as she pored over the computer manuals. It was only her head and shoulders because I couldn't do hands.

When she saw the picture, she caught her breath and brought her hands up in a steeple that brushed her lips. "Can I keep it?" she whispered.

"A present for your birthday tomorrow," I said. Then she had to go, but as she left, she scooted a pink note across to me:

now I know what's in your notebook.

On Friday a big car was parked outside the library. But I was only looking for Tracy, and there she was waiting for me in the door to the reading room. She was hugging her manuals and her notes in front of her. Her perfectness still made me blink. "Mother's outside," she said. "We'll go up to my house."

"Does she—"

"No. You'll be a surprise."

I followed her out. Would I have followed her anywhere? Then we were all three in the front seat. I was between them, but there was plenty of room.

"Mother, this is Molly Moberly, so now I can have a party."

When I looked at her mother, to be polite, she was perfect too. Her hand rested on the steering wheel in such a graceful way that I ached because I couldn't draw it. Her sudden smile lit up the car.

"How nice," she said, "but—"

"Mother, couldn't we cut just two slices out of the cake? Please?"

Tracy waited while her mother thought. Then with another sudden smile at me, Mrs. Pringle said, "Of course. Why not?" The car slid silently away, around the square and up the Lee Boulevard hill.

I knew the house before we turned into the drive. It was snow white with two bay windows and the last of the roses over the door. A perfect house without a leaf in the yard. Tracy's house.

Inside, it was better, everything pale, everything in place. A tinkling chandelier hung over the dining-room table. I thought we'd go straight up to Tracy's room. I was already drawing it in my head. But Tracy followed her mother into the kitchen. I supposed she wanted to be sure about the cake. It was a kitchen out of a dream, with marble counters. Her mother took three place mats out of a drawer that rolled out as quietly as the car. Then the three of us were at the dining-room table, Tracy across from me, her mother between us. We had milk with our cake, and there were napkins with lace edges that reminded me of the jacket Mrs. Voorhees wore to bed.

I copied Tracy to see how big a bite to fork out of the slice. Then I couldn't taste it. Mrs. Pringle's eyes were moving over me, scanning.

"Mother, Molly drew my picture," Tracy said. "For my present." So she hadn't shown it to her.

"Are you an artist, Molly?" Her mother had given herself a napkin but no cake, and she was folding it into neat pleats, like her skirt.

"I just draw," I said, looking down at the lace over my jeans knees. One of my hands rested on the table. I wanted her to see my manicure.

"And where do you live?"

I looked across at Tracy, wishing it was just the two of us. But she was looking back at me with her mother's eyes.

"With my great-aunt. Mrs. Moberly."

"Ah," Mrs. Pringle said. "I don't think I—"

"She's a practical nurse. She nurses old Mrs. Voorhees."

"Oh yes," Mrs. Pringle said. "On Park Place."

I was a rough-edged jigsaw-puzzle piece, and she wondered how to fit me in.

"And where are your mother and father?"

A clock ticked somewhere in the house while they both waited for an answer.

"My mother's in a hospital."

"How very sad." But Mrs. Pringle was looking at Tracy. "I believe your guest could manage another small slice of cake. Go out to the kitchen and get it. Use the server, and bring it in on a dessert plate, one that matches these."

I watched the whisk of Tracy's skirt as she went through the kitchen door. And I wondered what to do with Mrs. Pringle's next question, the one about my father, because I didn't have one. I had a question of my own. Could she really be Tracy's teacher in every subject? Did they put on gym shorts and divide up into two teams for P.E.? But no. It looked like Tracy and her mother were on the same team.

"Can I see Tracy's room?" I asked. The question popped out of nowhere, but I knew her bed would be made. I pictured stuffed animals on it.

"Oh, I don't know about that." But one of her sudden smiles changed Mrs. Pringle's face. "Yes, of course you may, and it gives me a very good idea."

Did I eat the second slice of cake? I don't remember, but then I was following them up the carpeted stairs to Tracy's room. There was a white canopy over a bed layered in white flounces, and again I thought about Mrs. Voorhees, her petticoats. It wasn't quite a girl's room. There weren't any stuffed animals, and the pictures on the walls were framed flowers. I'd supposed she'd have a phone of her own, a white one, but I didn't see it.

Mrs. Pringle opened up the doors to a wall of closets while Tracy stood back, looking away. My eyes jumped. There were so many clothes in there, all Tracy's, all on padded hangers and lots of them preserved in plastic. I didn't care about clothes, but I didn't know anybody had that many.

But then I saw they were all the clothes that Tracy had ever had. Some of them were a little girl's dresses, neatly arranged through the years. Mrs. Pringle stood back and touched her chin. Then her hand went forward. It was a plaid skirt, for autumn, a Tracy skirt.

"Tracy, turn your back," her mother said, "while Molly tries this on for size."

I didn't know what to think. I thought I could pull it on over my jeans, but her mother wouldn't let me. I didn't know if it fit or not. When had I had a skirt?

"You can turn around now, Tracy," Mrs. Pringle said. "Yes, I thought that one would suit you, Molly. Tracy's a little too tall for it now, and I couldn't do anything with the hem, not with those pleats."

I could feel them brushing my bare knees. Bare knees felt like summertime. I was wearing some sweatshirt, which was all wrong. Mrs. Pringle pointed at it. "But not bad," she said, "with a blouse under it."

Her fingers got busy going through the blouses.

They were all white or pastel with careful little collars. Tracy was ahead of me in blouse size too. Mrs. Pringle took one out. "Are you wearing underwear under that sweatshirt?" I nodded, so she helped me pull it over my head to try on the blouse. Then the sweatshirt went on again over it. She came up behind me, and I felt her hands at my neck, fixing the collar. She was dressing me. Did she dress Tracy every morning, in the clothes laid out the night before? Tracy hung there in the room, watching. It wasn't her party now.

Mrs. Pringle chose another skirt and two more blouses. She had a quick, neat way of folding them in the air. When she folded up my jeans too, I knew I was going to wear this skirt home. She was giving me these clothes, and that's why she'd let me see Tracy's room. "I'll just run you home in the car," she said.

"I can walk," I said. "And it's downhill."

"I couldn't take the risk," Mrs. Pringle said. "The things that go on in this town. It's full of people nobody knows now. It's getting to be like everywhere else."

On the way home I sat on the outside, not between them. I had to show Mrs. Pringle where Cedar Street was. I'd already thanked her for the clothes, though they were Tracy's. But I still didn't really know what had happened to me. I could only wonder at Tracy having this much mother when I didn't have any.

As we pulled up to Aunt Fay's house, Will was outside, leaning on a rake about as tall as he was. He'd done his grandma's yard. Now he was working on ours. It was almost worth it all to see his face when I stepped out of the big car in a skirt. His jaw dropped. When I turned to watch the car drive away, Tracy looked back to see this boy I knew. She smiled her mother's sudden smile.

"I was fixing to rake up a big bunch of leaves we could jump in," Will said, trying to rest his chin on top of the rake handle. "But I see you're not dressed for it."

"Certainly not," I said. "Couldn't think of it."

I went on up the porch steps, doing a little something extra with my hips to make the skirt whisk, though I still really didn't have hips.

I carried the bundle up through the empty house. In my room I stepped out of the skirt and pulled my sweatshirt over my head to get the blouse off. Then I dressed again in my own clothes, as if I'd never been to the Pringles'. Trying to use her mother's own graceful gestures, my hands arranged all Tracy's blouses and skirts in a dresser drawer on top of Arlette's bobby pins. There was something else I needed to know. Until I knew, I'd keep them here. I wasn't exactly hiding them.

But I jumped when the front door opened. I went out in the attic to the top of the stairs, and Aunt Fay was at the bottom, looking up. I didn't know why she was home now. But living with Debbie had taught me not to expect anything regular from adults. Aunt Fay was looking up at me, looking me over in a way she never did.

"I'm going to run up to Edith Voorhees's," she said. "You come."

This was only my second visit to Mrs. Voorhees. After the first time, I'd thought maybe Aunt Fay was going to take me with her every time she went, to keep an eye on me. But she hadn't.

This second visit was almost the same: the old lady in the bed with her face all painted up, a little cranky. This time she sent me off on errands all over the house, mostly looking for things I couldn't find, things she probably didn't even want.

The house was like a furniture store, everything nice but too much of it, so it was hard to find anything. Besides, the rooms were all dim even after you switched on a light. Aunt Fay gave her a shot in her behind, and Mrs. Voorhees yowled like a baby.

On the way home I said, "Doesn't she ever get up? Is she bedfast?"

"Edith?" Aunt Fay said. "She's up and dressed like Mrs. Astor's pet pony three mornings a week to go to the beauty parlor. If Rose can't take her, she calls a cab. I'm nearer bedfast than she is."

So I kept learning how old people act, and it was all new to me.

Will had bagged all the leaves from two yards. It was dark by now, but we saw him up on the McKinneys' front-porch roof framed in the light, trying to hang a storm window.

"Puts me in mind of the night before school started," Aunt Fay remarked, "when he come in your room off the back-porch roof."

Which made me jump, but she just kept busy, aiming the car.

Even Aunt Fay had combination screens and storms on her windows. But Will was wrestling with a big old wood storm window that made him stagger on the slant of the roof.

"Roll off," I'd told him the night he climbed up to my window, and now he looked like he might.

"Is Mrs. McKinney poor?" I asked, meaning the clunky old storm window, and the paint peeling off the house.

"Poor as Job's turkey," Aunt Fay said, "and getting poorer. They've got their Social Security, and that's about the size of it." She must have heard me thinking Mrs. McKinney was getting poorer since she had to feed Will, because she said, "He's good help for her. He's got a mouth on him, and he'll be a handful later. But he's a good boy."

When she'd swung around to the garage, she said she was going to look in on Wilma McKinney, so I went on up to the house. I took it for granted that I'd never get inside the McKinneys' house, and I guessed that was just the way some old people were.

It was pitch-dark when I came in our back door, but

I didn't flip on the kitchen light. I was halfway across the room when I knew I wasn't alone. I don't know what told me. But there was something extra in the room.

I looked toward the kitchen table, and a dark figure sat slumped in one of the chairs.

I wasn't a screamer, but I came close.

Chapter

6

⋮

My sneaker shrieked on the linoleum when I spun around. Instead of bolting outdoors like a sane person, I grabbed the wall to find the light switch. I guess I had to know.

I looked back in the dazzling light, and it was an old man, maybe the oldest man I'd ever seen. He didn't move. Maybe he couldn't, but that didn't help. I kept swallowing my heart.

He was slumped in the chair with his jaw dropped. He could be dead. He could be a dead body somebody left here. The door was never locked. But then something made him stir, maybe the light, maybe me. His eyes opened, and he looked up under the shock of white hair.

His neck shrank back from the buttoned collar on his work shirt. He wasn't dirty or anything, but he looked terrible, and he was looking at me. My mind whirled, but I had to know who he was. Was he one of those people who came to Aunt Fay because she was cheaper than a doctor's appointment? That had to be it, and it looked like he'd waited too late. I could hear him breathing, and it didn't sound good.

"Ruth Ann?" he said in a voice that echoed in the kitchen.

I felt the screen door at my back. I wanted to slide out into the night, but I edged into the room. One of his hands was on the table, loose like it didn't belong to him. His fingers were curled. The nails on them were thick and thorny. He needed a manicure bad. "Do you want to see Aunt Fay? Mrs. Moberly?"

"I want my supper is what I want." His voice was mushy, and you could see his teeth were false. They wobbled all over his mouth. "Where'd everybody go?" He looked around the empty kitchen. "It's suppertime. Look out the window, Ruth Ann. It's already as dark as the inside of a hog."

Now I was as near as the other kitchen chair, gripping the back of it. I was Ruth Ann, and he wanted his supper, and I didn't know what to do.

But then Aunt Fay's shoe hit the bottom porch step hard. She pounded up on the porch and banged the screen door open.

"Claude," she said, looking right at the old man.

Did he know her? He looked up, somewhat interested.

"Who is it?" I was still clinging to the chair back.

"It's Claude McKinney," Aunt Fay said. "Will's grandpa." Then her voice dropped a mile. "He don't know where he is a lot of the time." She strode around behind him and gripped him under his arms. "Claude, you had Wilma worried to death. She thought you was in the bed. You don't want to run around the neighborhood like that."

He made little moans as she hoisted him out of the chair. I had the screen door open when she steered him outside. "Where's my supper?" He reared back to give her an injured look. "Ruth Ann don't want to give me any."

"You've had your supper, Claude," she said. "Oyster stew and corn bread."

"Well, if I had it, I didn't know it," he said.

Now we were crossing the backyard and going through the McKinneys' gate. I was trying to get around them on the steps to open the screen door, but Aunt Fay said, "No, you wait outside."

Mrs. McKinney came up to the screen door and held it open. "It's all right. Let her come in," she said, meaning me. "Where was he?"

"He was in my kitchen."

"Oh law," Mrs. McKinney said. She wasn't in her nightgown. She was wearing a sweatsuit with the sleeves pushed up, and her hairnet. "Oh law."

"It could have been worse," Aunt Fay said. "He could have gotten out in traffic." Between them, they put him on a chair. The McKinneys' kitchen was about the same as Aunt Fay's except for all the medicine bottles on the drainboard. And the fact that Aunt Fay had a framed picture of Elvis on her kitchen wall, and Mrs.

McKinney only had calendars. I looked up, and Will was in the door to the front hall. He stood there with his hands braced on both sides of the door, watching. He didn't say anything, and neither did I. I thought Mrs. McKinney was trying to overlook me. But once they got Mr. McKinney settled, she glanced down at me and said, "Honey, did he give you a scare?"

"Not too bad," I said. "Who's Ruth Ann?"

She shook her head. "Oh well, that was his sister. That goes way back."

We left then. It was time to. Still, Will hung in the doorway to their front hall. I could feel his eyes on us as we left. When we were going out the door, Mr. McKinney said behind us, "Did I eat?"

Aunt Fay reached out for me as we made our way across the yards in the dark. Her hand felt heavy on my bony shoulder.

"That's why you go over to the McKinneys' a lot," I said.

"That's right. I go over to spell Wilma. She's got her hands full."

"It's not a job. You don't get paid."

"I wouldn't take pay from Wilma. And she'd be the same if it was the other way around. My man was sick before he died. Moberly. Wilma was right there for me. Anyway, her and me go way back. And Claude too. We had us some times when we was all young and hopeful." Her voice sounded different in the dark.

We went on in the house then, and she rustled us

up some supper. Oyster stew and corn bread. So that's why Will and I had the same lunch on the first day of school. Aunt Fay cooked for the McKinneys some because Mrs. McKinney had her hands full. Oh yes, I thought I knew everything then.

Only one thing lingered in my mind, hung there like a cobweb. When I'd come in the dark kitchen to find the figure at the table, I hadn't once thought it might be Debbie—Debbie come back to get me. It never crossed my mind, and that worried me.

I sat through school all that next Monday, not hearing a word said. All my thoughts galloped ahead to the last bell when I could run down to the library.

No car was idling outside when I got there, and my throat wasn't tight. I even took my time climbing the smoothed steps up to the front entrance. I didn't look ahead to see if Tracy was in the reading room. I was in no hurry to know.

She wasn't there, and the half of me that knew she wouldn't be felt smug and hard. I flopped down at the table anyway, scraping the chair. Would she be late? No, she never was. She wasn't coming, but I opened my homework and stared holes in it just to prove I wasn't there for Tracy.

Of course she hadn't come. Her mother wouldn't let her. Tracy had made a friend, a stray like me, so even the library wasn't safe for her. Now her mother would let her come to the library only during school hours, for safety's sake. I pictured the two of them sitting at their dining-room table this minute, Tracy in the kind of school clothes nobody really wore to school, doing her mother's assignments. I made myself sit in the reading room twenty-five minutes more before I let myself go home.

Aunt Fay and I had fallen into the habit of having supper together, late, after she came back from the McKinneys'. She even taught me a little about cooking, not much. It was mostly rooting around in her big deep freeze to take out things in time to thaw. She didn't have a microwave. She said it might cook her hand.

That Monday night after supper, I went up to Arlette's room and dug out all the clothes that Tracy's mother had given me. I carried them down to the kitchen where Aunt Fay was having a second cup of instant. She sat with her legs crossed in her way, with the ankle of one on the knee of the other and her ankle bracelet glittering. She'd put a sweet potato casserole in the oven, and it was beginning to smell good. She cooked whenever she could.

When I walked in with the pile of Tracy's clothes, Aunt Fay's eyebrows climbed up over her glasses. But she didn't say anything. I put the pile down on the kitchen table, but she just bided her time. Pretty soon she reached over and fingered the collar of a blouse. "What's this all about?"

"A lady gave them to me. Mrs. Pringle. I met her

daughter at the library, but she won't let her come there anymore."

"You could get some wear out of them." Aunt Fay felt one of the skirts. "They're better than what I could give you."

"They're not the kind of skirts they wear at school."

"But that one was a good fit on you."

That made me look up at her, and she was glancing my way. "I was over at Wilma McKinney's, and I seen you out of their upstairs window. You got out of that big car and sashayed past Will with all your skirttails twitching. Put me in mind of somebody."

"Who?"

"Edith Voorhees, when she was young."

We sat there with the clothes between us. "Tracy's mother only gave them to me to get rid of me."

"Are you too proud to take charity?" Aunt Fay looked around the room, away from me.

"No. I've taken charity before. You bought me about the first new clothes I ever owned. I'm used to castoffs. But I thought I'd made a friend, and I hadn't."

Aunt Fay nodded, but not at me.

Then after one of her long silent spells, she said, "Tell you what. Keep a skirt and a blouse to wear over to Edith Voorhees's. And we'll give the rest to Goodwill."

I looked at her, and something was happening to her mouth. It could have been a smile. "We'll give them to the poor," she said.

Chapter
7
.
.
.

The poem on Ms. Lovett's blackboard was called "November Night."

> Listen . . .
> With faint dry sound
> Like steps of passing ghosts,
> The leaves, frost-crisped, break from the trees
> And fall.

It was by a poet named Adelaide Crapsey, and I drew a Debbie in my notebook with autumn leaves caught in her hair.

Thanksgiving was coming, and Aunt Fay cooked around the clock in every spare minute. Cooking and baking and grating and freezing. I did some of it in an apron that swept the floor.

I supposed she was cooking for the McKinneys too. She was making enough for thrashers, as people said around here: a twenty-two-pound turkey and four pies. But then she said she was taking a Thanksgiving dinner to Mrs. Voorhees too. "She don't have anybody to eat with."

"Doesn't she have any friends?"

Aunt Fay turned over a floury hand. "You see how she is."

She cooked half the night before Thanksgiving, making up containers of dinner for everybody. Aunt Fay was the Queen of Tupperware.

When we got to Mrs. Voorhees's house the next morning, she sent me upstairs while she pulled the dinner together in the kitchen. I rapped on the bedroom door in Aunt Fay's way. When I went in wearing my Tracy blouse and skirt, Mrs. Voorhees squinted at me from the bed.

"Get out of here," she said. "I don't know you." When I was beside her, she said, "Oh, it's you. That's more like it. I suspected from the first day you were a girl." She meant the skirt, so I did a little twirl that she noticed. Then she put out her small paw to show me she hadn't been chipping away at her nail polish. "Are you wearing a bra yet?"

I thought that was too personal, but she said, "*I* wanted to wear a bra to first grade."

And I didn't doubt it.

Aunt Fay lumbered into the room. "Edith, I'm not hauling your Thanksgiving dinner up them stairs. You're not having it in bed. You can come downstairs in your wrapper."

"I wouldn't come downstairs in my wrapper if there was a tornado," she said.

"You'll think a tornado hit you if you don't get up off that bed and come down for your dinner." Aunt Fay started away, but Mrs. Voorhees liked having the last word.

"What about my shot?"

"You had your vitamin B12 shot already this month. You're not due."

And I was glad. I didn't even want to be in the room when Mrs. Voorhees got a shot. I didn't want to see the blood back up in the syringe. I'd seen that too often. I'd seen Debbie do that to herself.

"Well, I think I'm due for a shot," Mrs. Voorhees whimpered.

"You start losing track of time, and we'll have to make other arrangements for you," Aunt Fay said, and sailed out of the room.

Mrs. Voorhees glanced over at me. "She always did talk tough."

She sent me into her closet, and she had more clothes than Tracy Pringle. I hauled out every dress, winter and summer, before she found one that would do. For her stockings she pointed me to a chest of drawers. But at least she'd thrown back her covers and had both feet on the floor, fishing around for her bedroom slippers, which she called mules.

"Find my panty girdle."

A girdle? "But you're not fat," I said.

"It keeps everything in place," she said, so she was beginning to show some enthusiasm. She wanted a certain pin shaped like a gold leaf to wear on her dress. Her big white leather jewelry box stood on the top of the chest with bottles of perfume called Tabu and White Shoulders, names like that. There were several different framed pictures of several different men too.

The jewelry box was like buried treasure, everything tangled up in pearls and chains. Then I felt Mrs. Voorhees's eyes on me. Not her own. But behind the jewelry box was a silver-framed picture of herself taken long ago. You could see it was her, looking at me. Every hair was in place, and she was almost young, and as pretty as I figured. I lowered the lid to see, and she was holding a baby in her arms. A little baby dressed like a doll.

"Never mind about the pin if you can't find it," she said from across the room, snappish.

I didn't know where to look when she pulled the nightgown over her head and I had to hand her all her underclothes. "You should have seen my figure when I was twenty," she said.

Then she was dressed, reaching up to her shoulder where the gold pin should be, and up to touch her head. "My hair's a mess. Don't look at it." But I thought there were some other things I shouldn't have been looking at.

She was in her bathroom twenty minutes, and I

72

could smell the hair spray from here. When she came out, she was dressed and painted up like Mrs. Astor's pet pony.

She held on to my arm when we were going downstairs. We were the same height. "But you didn't put on shoes," I said. "You're wearing your mules."

"For heaven's sake," she said. "There's nobody here but Fay."

Aunt Fay had warmed up everything and arranged it on the dining-room table, using Mrs. Voorhees's fine china: the candied yams, the cranberry mold, everything in a pattern on a lace tablecloth and only the white meat of the turkey.

We three sat down at noon, and it was all new to me, the way things change here—the seasons and the frost-crisped leaves. And the way things never change. I kept thinking about what people here remembered, things like Thanksgiving and everybody's history—how Rocky Roberts's grandmother had to repeat fifth grade and the way Aunt Fay always talked tough. How every man in town wanted to marry Mrs. Voorhees and all the other old stories they talked out of shape.

And I thought about the doll baby Mrs. Voorhees held in the silver-framed picture and how she hadn't liked me looking at it.

We didn't get away early. Aunt Fay made a tray of turkey sandwiches for Mrs. Voorhees to have later because Rose had the day off. After that, we scrubbed down the whole kitchen. "If I leave a crumb," Aunt Fay said, "I'll hear about it."

At home we had to fix the McKinneys' dinner for Aunt Fay to carry over. I went upstairs to get out of Tracy's blouse and skirt. When I had one leg into my jeans, a thud shuddered through the house.

Down in the kitchen I found Aunt Fay on the floor. I could just see the frizz of her hair and the mound of her shoulder. She was almost under the table.

"Find my glasses," she said, grunting. "They flew off somewhere."

"What about *you*?"

"It's my bad leg." I could tell she was hurting, and gasping to keep from letting on. "I come down on it wrong. It just takes one false step."

She always limped, but it seemed a part of her.

"Help me up in that chair." Somehow I got her there. When I found her glasses, she hooked them over her ears like that solved everything.

"What if your leg's broken?"

"It's not broken. I just lit on it wrong." She tried to get up and fell back into the chair. "You'll have to deal with the McKinneys' dinner. I've got the oven on already."

For most of an hour she had me warming up and dishing up. I tried to fit everything in a grocery-store box I could barely budge. When she started to get up again, I saw she thought she was going to carry all this stuff over to the McKinneys herself.

I put a hand on her shoulder to keep her still, and she said, "We could get Will to come over and—"

"No, I'll take it," I said.

She winced and rubbed at her leg, and I hustled the big box out the back door. "Did you get the celery?" she said, and yes, I had.

I ought to have made two trips. The gate was un-latched, which helped. Then I went in the McKinneys' backward, dragging the box over the threshold. I turned around in the kitchen, and there sat Mr. Claude McKinney, slumped. He didn't look any better, but at least he was in his own kitchen. He may have smelled Thanksgiving, because he looked up, interested. Oh great, I thought. Now I have to be Ruth Ann.

"You that little girl from next door?"

He blinked his old pinkish eyes at me, and there was a spark of something in them. "My name's Molly," I said.

"Your name'll be mud if you didn't bring me some supper."

I took out the containers, hot and cold, and lined them up on the counter, next to all the medicine bot-tles. I turned the oven on warm since it didn't look like the McKinneys were ready to sit down.

"I could go ahead and eat right out of the pan," Mr. McKinney said.

"You try that," I said, "and you'll think a tornado hit you." I was the grown-up here. "Where is every-body?"

"They's all upstairs," he said.

A paper tablecloth with turkeys and pilgrims was on the kitchen table. "Where are your plates and silverware?" I said.

"Just where they always are," Mr. McKinney said, and I found them in cupboards and drawers. I set the table for him and Will and Mrs. McKinney, and he watched every move I made.

"You're a busy little body," he said. "Where's your grandpa?"

"I don't have one," I said. "Never did."

He thought about that. "You must have. You ought to look around for him. Sometimes we get away."

I put the cranberry mold in the center of the table because the refrigerator was full of more medicine. I stood back to check out my work, and now Mr. McKinney was sitting at his place with a paper napkin stuck in his collar.

Then something terrible happened. A sound tore through the McKinneys' house, from upstairs. A voice screaming up out of somebody or something. I didn't know if it was human. It wasn't words. It was an awful wail that filled the house.

Then nothing, like it hadn't happened.

I looked at Mr. McKinney, but he was just fiddling with his silverware, though he wasn't deaf. I couldn't remember being this scared before. I made a run for the back door. I wasn't even supposed to be in this house. Aunt Fay didn't want me here.

But I turned back. "Mr. McKinney, don't go near the stove because it's hot." Then I was out of there, into the dark, running for home like something was after me.

I felt skinned with fear, and Aunt Fay was watching me as I plunged in through our back door. She hadn't moved, but she'd hitched up her pant leg to rub the shin she'd fallen on. Because it was Thanksgiving, she hadn't worn her nurse's whites today. She was in the peach-colored pantsuit, which was her best. We looked at each other, but the ceiling light glinted on her glasses and hid her eyes.

"You don't just help out a little with the cooking at the McKinneys', do you?" I said. "You do it all."

"Pretty nearly," she said.

"And you spend a lot of time there every day. You don't just look in on Wilma McKinney."

"All the time I can give them," Aunt Fay said.

"There's somebody else in their house. Somebody besides Will and Claude and Wilma."

"That's right," she said, in a voice so flat I didn't know it.

Any other kid would have nagged her to know. But I didn't know how to nag or whine or whatever kids do. If I'd ever tried that on Debbie, she'd have turned away and gone away and not been there.

"Don't say anything to anybody," Aunt Fay said. "Don't let on. Don't ask Will."

Chapter
8
:

*U*nder the eaves in the attic, I'd found a card table and a folding chair. I could put them back when I left.

But now I set the table up in Arlette's room, below the window where Will came in that time. It was where I went since I didn't go to the library anymore. I drew a lot, and my notebook only had a few pages to go. I was working on a picture of Debbie in a sleigh because winter was on the way: Debbie in a velvet cape with a hood and fur around her face. A Christmas-card Debbie with her hands in an ermine muff, because I can't do hands. I was giving Debbie till Christmas Day to come for me. I knew it was a game, but I was playing it to win.

The only Christmas I knew anything about was whatever they did at school, and in some schools they didn't do much. But here they were making big plans.

The mixed chorus rehearsed through December. You could hear "The Holly and the Ivy" all over school. Every last one of us had it memorized. At the beginning of the school year the Kiwanis Club had donated instruments for an orchestra that tooted and sawed all month. If anybody went for tryouts, there were going to be solos and skits too. Will went.

I tried to hold back Christmas like I'd tried to hold back the first day of school. Then Ms. Lovett called me up after class one day. Some of my notebook Debbies were beginning to look like her. I hadn't seen my mother since summer.

"Have you thought about the program they'll hand out to the audience?" Ms. Lovett asked, and I just shrugged. I didn't know where she was going with this. "It will just be a piece of plain paper folded over unless you design the cover."

Then I saw I was supposed to draw something because she thought I was an artist. "I may not even be here by the time—"

"Then stop by after school today," she said.

She was trying to get me involved. I'd run into a teacher or two like that, other places, and I could usually keep my distance. But this was Ms. Lovett, and I'd been in the same school now for three months. "Is this an assignment?"

"Yes," she said, and her somewhat sad eyes brightened.

The show was on the last afternoon before Christmas vacation. Several people cut out, but parents came, so the auditorium filled up. I was there, wearing Tracy's blouse and skirt, because I'd heard the rumor people were dressing up even if they weren't on the stage. I had to hand out the programs as part of Ms. Lovett's assignment.

I'd done a mistletoe border and a red bow to frame the words WINTER WONDERLAND on the front page. Ms. Lovett had run off the programs on a color printer, and she'd made me sign my work. I hid my initials in among the mistletoe, but I kept looking at my handiwork as I gave out the programs. I'd never done anything that wasn't Debbie, except for the picture of Tracy, and that didn't count.

Mrs. McKinney came, so I knew Aunt Fay was at the McKinneys' house, holding the fort. She slipped into a seat at the back, keeping her coat on.

The orchestra struck up that song about the twelve days of Christmas, though they made it sound like a month. The curtains parted for some solos. Then the mixed chorus trooped onto risers and did "The Holly and the Ivy," which turned into a sing-along because we all knew it.

Rocky Roberts was stage manager. He'd been in and out of school all month, and when he was in my vicinity, he was always looking the other way. They'd tried to involve him by putting him in charge of drawing the curtain. He'd gotten it open, but now as the mixed chorus was winding up "The Holly and the Ivy," invisible Rocky pulled the wrong rope, and down came the movie screen. It thundered toward the stage like a garage door and knocked the entire back row of the mixed chorus, all boys, off the risers. They were gone in a flash.

Some people thought we were going to have a movie, but the adults jumped up—the teachers and Mr. Russell and all the parents of the back row. It could have been a mistake. Rocky said later it was.

So we had a long intermission. Some of the back row had to go to Miss Throckmorton's office to have their heads looked at. But the show went on, though they had to step it up because the buses were waiting. The mixed chorus was all girls now, performing right at the front of the stage to be on the safe side.

I knew Will had been working up something, but I didn't know what. And he'd had to stand up to Nelson Washburn because it wasn't cool for boys to go out for this kind of thing. Then Will strolled onto the stage.

Where the costume came from I never knew. He was between Santa's helper and a street person. He wore a cap with bells and a suit striped like a bumble-bee, and the toes of his boots curled up at the end. He came on ringing a big bell and carrying a box of matches, and he blinked out at the audience like he hadn't been expecting us. This got a laugh and some hoots, and he cocked his head to hear. Then in a big soprano voice he sang a sort of song:

"Christmas joys
And Christmas toys

For all the girls and all the boys—
Is this what Christmas is?"

He clanged his bell and looked out at us, inquiring.

"Holy nights
And fir-tree lights
And voices rising to the heights—
Old carols sung,
Green garlands hung,
And all the choirs giving tongue—
Is this what Christmas is?"

"Yes!" everybody yelled back at him, getting into it.
Now he dropped onto the floor and opened his box of
matches, showing us.

"I'm a little match boy huddled in the cold,
Begging for alms from young and old.
Could you give me just a penny?
Because believe me, folks, I haven't any.
'Tis the season for holly, the season for ivy,
But personally I'm not feeling so lively—
Is this what Christmas is?"

Now he was on his feet.

"I'm not sure in these hard times.
I'm not even sure if this dumb thing rhymes."

8 2

He cracked the heels of his elf boots in the air and did a dance off the stage.

It got a big round of whistling and foot stomping, though Ms. Lovett sat there, stunned. At least nobody doubted that he'd written it himself. There was no time for an encore, so we didn't get to hear "Achy, Breaky Heart."

Will was the last act, and Mrs. McKinney went out past me saying, "I thought he done real good." But long, long afterwards I could always get a rise out of him just by murmuring, "I'm a little match boy huddled in the cold."

Aunt Fay tried an elastic thing on her leg to give her support, though she said it was more trouble than it was worth. In the evenings I was an extra pair of hands and legs while we cooked for Christmas. Every time I pulled a long sheet of cookies out of the oven, I hoped I wouldn't be here to eat any.

Later, I remembered the cinnamon smell and the heat that wavered up over Elvis's face until we had to prop the back door open. The two of us moved from counter to stove, from table to sink, not saying much, just being together. Except in my mind I was upstairs throwing things into a suitcase, though I didn't have a suitcase.

I picked out nut meats and helped measure the ingredients for a pudding Aunt Fay steamed in a cheesecloth bag. Since the brandy was down from the top shelf, she set up a row of washed medicine bottles to fill with her own cough formula: brandy and honey and some pills she ground up for it, since head-cold season was coming. She set aside some bottles for the McKinneys.

I crossed off each night on the calendar in my mind. Then it was the night before Christmas Eve, and I was rolling out the slick dumplings. We were planning to bake two chickens to divide between Mrs. Voorhees and the McKinneys. I was wound tight from waiting for Debbie.

The sweat was pouring off both of us. Aunt Fay wiped the steam off her glasses with the tail of her apron. "I don't have you anything for Christmas," she said.

"That's all right." It crossed my mind that I might have made a picture as a gift for her. It didn't have to be a Debbie. Just some drawing she could stick up on the icebox after I was gone. "Anyway, you got me the coat."

She got me a coat when the weather turned because I didn't have anything for cold. I picked a puffy jacket that looked like what they wore at school.

"Well, I wanted to get you something else," she said. "But I haven't had a chance to look up. And getting these groceries together like to wipe me out. I don't know what. Maybe some nice soap."

She didn't know what a girl would want for Christmas, and, really, I didn't either. "It's okay," I said. "I may not be here."

I thought that was all right to say because I'd cost her quite a bit, and I couldn't pay her back. When Debbie came, she wouldn't be able to pay either because Debbie never could. Money ran through her hands and up her arms.

But something sudden came over Aunt Fay. She fussed her glasses back onto her face and sat down in such a heavy way, I thought her leg had given out again. A second passed, like a heartbeat. Then she said, "Never mind them dumplings. Put the potatoes on the fire. Then come over here and set down."

I put them on to boil. We were going to make two pans of escalloped, and I hurried because there was something urgent here. When I turned back, she was sitting with one hand bunching up the oilcloth on the table.

I hovered, not sitting. Looking at the stove, not at me, she said, "Molly, your mother isn't coming back for you at Christmas. I know it was a deadline in your mind, and I blame myself for not saying something sooner."

I watched her, dry-eyed because she had more to tell.

"Debbie isn't in that hospital place anymore. They couldn't keep her any longer, or she discharged herself."

"How do you know?"

"They called and told me."

"Maybe she's on her way here." I looked out in the hall like I could hear a car at the curb, her footstep on the porch.

"They called in October."

I went a little deaf, a little blind. All I could see was that stupid calendar in my mind. Every crossed-off day had taken Debbie farther away, not brought her nearer. Had I known it all along? How much of me had known?

"I looked for her in the days after that, in case she turned up," Aunt Fay was saying. "You never know. I didn't let on to you. I didn't want you to get keyed up, but I shouldn't have let it ride. I shouldn't have left it till Christmas."

But my mind was back in the fall, framing Debbie's face with autumn leaves. I saw her walking out of that hospital place, that facility, all those weeks ago with just her backpack. I watched her walk away, going nowhere and thinking she was free because she didn't have anyplace to be, glad to be out of that place so she could go look for junk because she was an addict. But she wasn't addicted to me.

I had the back of the kitchen chair in a grip, trying to hurt my hands. If I'd wanted her enough, would she have come? Had I gotten too comfortable here? I didn't mean to.

I saw us tonight, the way we'd be if she'd come for me. I'd be sitting up watching *Nightline* if we were in a motel, waiting for Debbie to find her way home—stoned or skinned up or smiling and throwing money on the bed.

I was crazy that night, so I had these visions. I could even jump out of my skin and look back at me. I saw me through Aunt Fay's eyes, and it was the same me who'd washed up here last summer, stringy and hungrier than I let on and too scared to be mad. I was back where I started.

"Was I wrong not to tell you sooner?" Aunt Fay said, her eyes finding mine, and me back in my skin again.

I had sense enough to tell her she wasn't wrong. I'd lost some time, dreaming the wrong dream. But what did that matter now? This was the closest we'd been, though the table was between us. "Would you have any idea where she went?" Aunt Fay said, quiet.

The four winds and anybody. I shook my head.

"But it wasn't just the drugs she needed." The words tumbled out of me. "She needed people to like her."

I wasn't enough. But I couldn't say that where anybody else could hear.

"That's right." Aunt Fay nodded. "That was Debbie. She was always hungry for someone to like her."

She said *like*, not *love*. Aunt Fay never said *love*. Some words are too dangerous to use. "Maybe someday she'll—"

"Maybe," I said. But I couldn't go on listening for footsteps on the porch. It was like one of those games you play as a kid, and one day, all of a sudden, the game doesn't work anymore. You're just running in circles. Or you're hiding and nobody's seeking you.

So I couldn't be twelve now, not after tonight. I'd been twelve too long.

"Can I stay here with you?"

Aunt Fay jerked, like I'd come up behind her. She looked at the stove. "There's a lot I can't do for you," she said. "But you're home."

You notice I didn't cry. Not that night. I'll tell you when.

Chapter

9

:
:
:

*C*hristmas Eve we headed up the hill with Mrs. Voorhees's dinner. It was sleeting and pitch-dark at five-thirty. When we pulled up to the house, lights twinkled in the overgrown living-room window.

"Would you look at that," Aunt Fay said. "She's made Rose put up a tree. She's gotten herself overstimulated. She'll be barking at the moon all night. I'll have to give her a saline shot."

"What good will that do?"

"It won't do anything. But it hurts worse than her B12 shot, so she likes it better."

When we came through the front door with the dinner, Mrs. Voorhees was at the foot of the curving stairs, posing. She was dressed in her Christmas best. It was a green taffeta that went to the floor with pearls at her neck. She was swinging a fine black-and-silver cane, pointing it to show off the Christmas tree winking in the living room.

"Is that cane my Christmas present?" Aunt Fay said,

hustling in the chicken and dumplings. "Because I'm the one with the leg."

Mrs. Voorhees made big eyes and pursed up her red rosebud mouth. "A woman of your weight leaning on this cane would snap it like a twig."

"Before you get too ornery to live," Aunt Fay said, handing off the chicken to me, "I'm going to give you a saline shot. We'll get that over with before we eat."

"A saline shot!" Mrs. Voorhees said like she'd never heard of one. "Fay, I'm not going to stump back upstairs and get on the bed dressed like this so you can use me for a pincushion."

"No need for that," Aunt Fay said, moving in on her. "You can just hike them skirts and bend over the banister. Because, girl, you've got a shot coming."

It was their way of exchanging Christmas greetings, so I brought in the rest of our dinner from the car and laid it all out in the kitchen—the pan of escalloped potatoes, the green-bean-and-mushroom-soup casserole, the jar of gravy, the Waldorf salad, the crescent rolls, and the steamed pudding with hard sauce.

We ate by candlelight, and I'd only seen people do that in pictures. Four tall white candles—*tapers*, Mrs. Voorhees called them—in fancy glass holders. And in the middle of the table a white poinsettia plant. I'd never seen a white poinsettia before. It didn't look quite real, but then maybe Christmas isn't supposed to be.

We sat there in the candlelight, having our Christmas. At one end Mrs. Voorhees, shimmering green, was already slipping a second crescent roll out of the silver basket. Aunt Fay in her peach pantsuit was planted at the other end, and the candle flames reflected in her glasses. It was a good dinner. Even Mrs. Voorhees said so, and I remembered that line in the song Will the Little Match Boy sang: "Is this what Christmas is?"

I decided it must be. The best part was not counting the days and waiting for Debbie anymore. Oh, I wasn't over Debbie. I don't mean that. You don't just let go when you've been hanging on all your life. Everything felt different though, and it wasn't just Christmas. I can't explain it, but if somebody came in this dining room now and took a picture of us, I knew I'd be in it.

"Just put a little dab on my plate," Mrs. Voorhees said when we brought in the pudding. "And a dab of hard sauce. I don't know where I'll put that much."

"Beats me," Aunt Fay muttered out in the kitchen. "If she didn't have that panty girdle on, she'd explode. Five crescent rolls. She's got more stomachs than a Holstein cow."

We'd just finished up the pudding when the phone rang. Mrs. Voorhees was chasing one final raisin around her plate with a dessert fork. Aunt Fay slipped out to answer in the kitchen.

When I caught Mrs. Voorhees cocking an ear to hear, she said, "Well, it could be for me, you know. This is my house."

But Aunt Fay didn't come back, and we heard snatches of her end of a conversation.

"You say he's not bringing up any phlegm?"

"One of her other patients," Mrs. Voorhees whispered. "Another poor sufferer."

There was more we couldn't hear, but then Aunt Fay said, "Call the pharmacist and tell him you want an oxygen concentrator. Tell him I'll pick it up on the way. No, I've had my dinner. It's all right. I'll be there directly."

She came up behind my chair, and Mrs. Voorhees said to her, "You don't mean you have to—"

"Yes," Aunt Fay said. "I've got an emergency." Her hand fell on my shoulder. "Edith, will you have Molly to stay overnight?" She squeezed my shoulder, meaning she wanted me to play along. She wanted me to keep Mrs. Voorhees company. Because it was Christmas Eve maybe, or to keep her from barking at the moon.

It was still only a little after eight when I finished up in the kitchen. I'd been on my own in there, cleaning up from our meal. Mrs. Voorhees had gone straight upstairs, saying, "All that heavy food is the last thing a person in my condition should be eating."

So I had the kitchen to myself, getting the leftovers back in the Tupperware and washing up by hand. Mrs. Voorhees didn't want her china or her crystal run through the dishwasher. Then I dried everything to a high polish, because if I left a spot on a glass, I'd hear about it.

It wasn't an up-to-date kitchen, not like the one at Tracy Pringle's house. The countertops had linoleum on them, and the dinette set was old chrome. But Mrs. Voorhees wouldn't have spent much time in here. I seemed to know things about her, how she'd always gotten other people to do for her. It was like a talent, and she was talented that way.

I didn't mind the work. Wasn't I always pretending I had an apartment in some city with a kitchenette? And here I had a full kitchen. But something nagged at me, something new.

The sleet was hitting the black kitchen window, and I kept thinking about Aunt Fay skittering down the slick hill in the Dart and having to make a stop at the pharmacy. She wasn't that great a driver either. Before last night I hadn't worried about her, hadn't thought much about her when she wasn't there. And she was in and out. But now I stewed some, wondering if she was all right. And that was new.

I arranged some of her star-shaped sugar cookies on a plate to take up to Mrs. Voorhees for later. Then I ran a damp rag over all the countertops and behind the toaster.

I supposed I'd better shut off the lights on the Christmas tree in the living room. They were all pink, and the glass balls were either pink or silver, and up close you could see the tree was artificial. It was the

Mrs. Voorhees of trees. I sat down on a needlepoint settee to admire it. I sat there as long as I dared, watching the tree wink pink and letting some more Christmas happen. Then I pulled the plug and went on upstairs.

Mrs. Voorhees was sitting in her bed as usual, watching the door. She wore a flannel nightgown with her hair tied up in a gauzy scarf. "You took your time," she said. "What did you do, scrub the pattern off the plates? What have you got there, cookies for Santa? Bring them over and put them on this bedside table where he'll find them."

Oh yes, she was going to be restless tonight. As Aunt Fay said, her only ailment was lack of exercise.

"Have you thought where you're going to sleep?" Her voice came out of nowhere. She'd cold creamed her face, so she had no mouth or eyelashes. I thought there must be plenty of bedrooms where I could sleep.

"You better bunk in here with me so you won't get scared in the night."

"I don't get scared in the night."

"You never stayed in a haunted house before."

"Is this place haunted?"

She waved a little paw. "Common knowledge."

"Who's haunting it?"

"I am!" she said. "Just a joke. But you can pull that rollaway out of the back of the closet and sleep at the foot of my bed."

So that's where she wanted me to be. She lent me

one of her nightgowns because we were pretty nearly the same size. "I don't have an extra toothbrush for you," she said as I was making up the rollaway bed. "But I guess your teeth won't drop out. And here, you might as well just finish off these cookies."

There were only two left, and she'd made it sound like I'd eaten all the others.

I'd asked Aunt Fay what hospital corners were, and now I had the chance to show Mrs. Voorhees I knew. She watched my every move. She was bright-eyed and bushy-tailed.

"You've made up that bed tighter than the envelope on a love letter," she said. "You'll have to tear it up to get into it."

But I had the feeling we weren't near bedtime. "Are you going to be able to sleep?" I asked her.

"Sleep?" She was astonished. "I haven't been able to sleep since 1958. If I *slept*, I'd think I was in a coma. I nod off. That's the best I can do. It's Christmas Eve. Are you going to hang up your stocking?"

"I'm too old for that."

"Then quit fiddling with that bed and bring me my jewelry box."

I blinked. "You wear your jewelry overnight?" I wouldn't put it past her.

"Just go get it."

It weighed a ton, and I was careful lifting it so I wouldn't knock over the perfume bottles. I noticed the silver-framed picture of her and the doll baby wasn't there. When I brought the box over to the bed, she was patting a place beside her where I was to put it down, and myself too.

Raising the lid, she peered into her pirate treasure. Now our heads were close, because that much of anything amazed me. "I remember every dress I wore with this stuff," she said. "You can poke around. Look at that sunburst. Voorhees brought that to me from Chicago when he was up there at a Masonic meeting." It probably wasn't diamonds, but it looked like diamonds. It was blinding. "Pearls are nice too," she said. "Very flattering."

We both poked around, untangling the pearls and matching up the earrings, making an evening of it. Finally she said, "Well, don't you see anything you like?"

I didn't know what she meant. I guess I liked it all. "Girls like jewelry," she said, but I just sat there, not knowing.

"Pick yourself out something you like. For heaven's sake, it's Christmas."

I stared at her. She wanted to give me a present. What if I picked the sunburst pin? It was bigger than my chest.

"Never mind," she said. "I'll find you something." She reached in and pulled out a gold chain, and she knew just where it was. It was so delicate, it was almost not there. On it hung a tiny ring, like a baby would wear. She held it up, and it glittered like tinsel. "Twenty-four karat," she said.

It was the plainest thing in the box, and the best. "Let's try it on you, see how it looks."

It was so fine and light, I could hardly feel it around my neck. "That's what we call important jewelry," she said. "Real gold and simple enough to wear all the time. Go look at yourself in the mirror."

The room was full of mirrors. All her closet doors were mirrors. I didn't like looking at myself, but I looked at the chain with the little ring on it, caught up on the collar of the flannel nightgown. "You could wear it next to your skin," she said from the bed. "You wouldn't ever need to take it off."

So I had a Christmas present this year, an important piece of jewelry I'd never have to take off. When we got settled in our beds, Mrs. Voorhees was snoring in two minutes. But I stayed awake, feeling the gold chain around my neck, feeling the baby's ring nestled at my throat.

Rose was coming the next morning to take Mrs. Voorhees home with her, to have Christmas Day with her family. I mentioned that there were plenty of leftovers for when she got home.

"They'll eat their heads off all day long at Rose's," she said. "After that, I won't be able to look food in the face."

I'd thanked her twice for the gold chain, once last night and now again this morning when I'd taken up her breakfast. She just shrugged, but said, "You can drop in any time. You don't have to wait for Fay. I may have something else for you—I don't know what."

But she didn't have to give me things to get me to come. "What are you giving Rose for Christmas?" I said to change the subject.

"A check for twenty-five dollars and my last year's coat. I just as well give away all my coats. I don't get out." But she was already over at the closet, deciding what to wear to Rose's all-day Christmas dinner.

I walked home, down the hill on Christmas morning, avoiding the slick spots. The sleet had coated the yards so it was almost a white Christmas. Nobody was out yet. People were indoors, opening their presents. Not a car went by all the way to the square, and there was only truck traffic on Jefferson. It was nice without anybody around. I felt like I owned the town.

Though it was already ten-thirty when I got home, I looked over the back of the couch to make sure Aunt Fay wasn't asleep on it. I glanced in her bedroom too, but it looked unslept in.

Nothing warned me all the way up the attic stairs, but when I went into Arlette's room, somebody was asleep in my bed. I jumped a foot. It was Will.

10

.
.
.

*H*e sat straight up. He had on somebody else's wool shirt, and I wondered if he was wearing anything else. His hair was in his eyes and standing up in a halo at the back of his head.

"What time is it?"

"Time you got out of my bed," I said, being cool. Careful too. It felt risky to ask him why he was here. I stood by the door, fingering my invisible chain inside my puffy jacket.

He scratched his scalp. ". . . Since you were at Mrs. Voorhees's, your aunt Fay sent me over here to sleep."

He didn't say why.

"I've got to go," he said, which could mean a couple of things.

"Bathroom's downstairs," I said. "You wearing anything but that shirt? Should I hide my eyes?" His clothes were in a puddle on the floor next to a pair of small cowboy boots I hadn't seen before. He threw back my covers, and he was wearing pajama bottoms.

"I don't have an extra toothbrush," I said, "but I guess your teeth won't drop out."

He trudged past me, sleepy and sulky, heading for the bathroom with his boots in his hand.

I thought I'd better give him breakfast, because I didn't know what was going on next door at the McKinneys'. I boiled water for instant oatmeal and threw in a handful of raisins. I poured out a glass of juice and fixed a plate of Christmas cookies.

"Merry Christmas," I said when he came into the kitchen, swaying in the boots.

"Yeah," he said.

I hung around by the sink, letting him eat, not asking anything because being Will, he couldn't keep quiet forever.

"Your aunt Fay and my grandma kind of got into it last night."

"Into what?"

"Well, they had a big disagreement, and then they sent me over here to sleep."

I waited a little and then said, "That's the shortest story I ever heard."

"I didn't want to come over here," he mumbled. "I'd sooner have stayed there. I'm not a kid."

"What were they fussing about? Was it about taking care of your grandpa?"

"Yeah." His head hung low, and his eyes were on the oilcloth. "It was your aunt Fay spouting off. She wanted to put him in the hospital."

"Aunt Fay doesn't spout off," I said. "She says what she thinks, and she's trained."

"Whatever," he said.

"How bad is he?" I said. "Your grandpa."

"It's pneumonia. He's had it before. But they got this thing from the drugstore. It sucks in room air and blows out double the oxygen. It helps him breathe."

"But maybe at the hospital they could—"

"Don't look at me," Will said. "I wanted him to go."

There was something not real about this conversation. So I said, "New boots? Christmas?"

He nodded. You could hear the boots creaking under the kitchen table. "They're from my dad."

"He sent them to you?"

"That's right. I better get going."

He was scraping back from the table, but something made me say, "Wait a minute. I want to tell you something."

I came over and sat down in the other chair so he wouldn't get up.

"What?" he said, like he didn't want to hear.

"You were right."

"What about?"

"About my mother. She's not coming back for me."

"I never said—"

"I know, but remember that time you said maybe I wouldn't be staying and maybe I would? You figured I would."

Will sat there, fooling with a spoon, making half-moons in the oilcloth with it.

"Well, I'm staying," I said.

"That's good," he said. "You okay with that?"

I nodded.

"Maybe someday your mom will—"

"Maybe. Maybe not. You know why I told you? It hurts to say it out loud. You know why I did?"

"Because we're two of a kind?"

"I don't know about that, but I told you something I wouldn't want anybody else to know. Not anybody."

"Well," he said, "I . . . appreciate it."

"I leveled with you."

"Okay," he said. "That was good."

"So you can level with me. It's not your grandpa who has pneumonia, is it? It's not Claude." Could I always tell when Will was lying, or was it just this one time?

He tried to get out of it. He looked all around the kitchen ceiling before he said, "No. Grandpa's okay. Not okay, he doesn't know where he is, but he doesn't have pneumonia. It's not him who has it."

"Then who?"

The doorknob rattled, and Aunt Fay came in from the back porch. I wouldn't have recognized her if I'd met her at Marshalls. Her face was gray, and her eyes were red and swollen. She usually looked tired, but this morning she was way past that.

She leaned back against the closed door. Will was coming out of his chair. "How is he?"

"He's breathing a little easier," she said. "He's getting some rest."

Will sat back down, and Aunt Fay watched us both.

"I was fixing to tell Molly," Will said to her.

She gave him a long look, and said, "Don't let me stop you."

"It's my dad who has pneumonia," Will said. "He didn't send me here. We came together, on a bus. We been sharing the spare room upstairs at Grandma and Grandpa's since we got here. Except he was so sick last night they didn't want me in the room."

Part of me knew every word just before he spoke it. I remembered Thanksgiving night when I went over there and—

"We came here," Will said, "because my dad got sick. He lost his job and got sicker. Then we ran out of money, and he came home and brought me with him."

"Pneumonia," I said. "You said he'd had it before."

"That's right."

Aunt Fay was behind Will's chair now. She had a hand on his shoulder, and it always meant something when she did that. She didn't touch you for nothing.

Time passed, and nobody said anything. You could have heard bees if it was summer. Way in the distance a train hooted, and you only ever heard that at night. I chanced a look at Will, and his eyes were full to over-flowing.

"You want to go on home now?" Aunt Fay said. "You don't have to."

"I want to go," he said in a low voice. "I've had my say."

"That's it?" Aunt Fay said. "That's what you wanted Molly to know?"

He nodded. Then he went on home, and it was just the two of us.

"You told me his dad was in jail," I said.

"No I didn't. I said that's what they say."

I could have asked her more, but not while she was looking at me like that. Maybe I didn't want to know. I'd said I couldn't be twelve any longer, but I still was.

"I've got to get me some sleep," she said, "or I'll break down on Christmas Day."

She moved as slow as I'd ever seen her, limping out of the kitchen and up the hall, still in her peach pantsuit from last night. She went in the living room to get on the couch because she'd never get in her bed during the day.

New Year's Eve came, and that was the time Mrs. Voorhees taught me to play gin rummy with her bed for a card table. But we didn't play for money. I wasn't that dumb. Then it was January, and now I could say I'd been here since last year.

I saw even less of Will than I had before Christmas, so I was slow to notice something happening to him. We both turned thirteen that winter, but it hit him harder.

It must have been coming on him in stages, but I didn't notice till February. Then I couldn't believe it. I looked up at him one day, and I was looking up at him. He was taller than Nelson Washburn. I looked down, and his new gym shoes were like boats. He couldn't have gotten three weeks of wear out of those cowboy boots. Blond though he was, you could see a whisper of whisker under his nose. His neck was filling out, and I thought he had a cold he couldn't shake off before I realized his voice was changing. Girls stopped looking over his head.

One day he was the Little Match Boy, and the next he was a guy. It was amazing. But I saw him mostly from afar. His new legs gave him a long stride, and he was always striding in the other direction. Nowadays he had lunch over at Nelson's table.

I figured it out in math class one day. You have to have something to think about in math class. It struck me that Will and I never had been two of a kind. I was the only one sent here by somebody who couldn't keep me and didn't want to. We weren't strays like us. I was just a stray like me.

Will came here with his dad. Maybe his dad was a secret in the attic. I suppose I thought he'd broken out of jail. But Will had more family here than I did. He had a stake in this town. He'd been easing in all along. By high school he'd be another Nelson Washburn, just not so rich and stuck on himself. Besides, these things are easier for a boy. Will would belong here, and I'd only hang on the edges and watch.

It was pretty sad, but now that I was thirteen, I liked sad stories. I just wished they weren't about me.

Chapter

11

. . .

Something woke me in the middle of the night, some sound from the street. It wasn't morning yet, and I was glad. There was going to be a test in science, and I was in no hurry. The house below me felt empty. Aunt Fay hadn't been home when I went to bed.

I woke again in the daylight, and the house was still empty. Down in the kitchen I put on a pot of coffee for her when she got there. As I was making my lunch to take, her car pulled into the garage. She came in the back door as gray-faced as at Christmas. "Are you going to be late for school?" That was small talk, and she didn't make small talk.

"No, I'm okay."

She sat down in her coat, and I poured her out a mug. Winter had gone on too long, and the wind went right through you.

"Fred died." She took the mug in both hands. "Will's dad."

I just stood there. I hadn't thought about death. How could he die with Aunt Fay on his case? It wasn't real to me. Will's dad wasn't real. I'd never seen him.

"He died in the paramedic van on the way to the hospital. Will was in the van with him. I followed in my car with Wilma and Claude because we couldn't leave Claude. Then by the time we got to the emergency room, it was all over."

I couldn't think what to ask first. "Did you know?"

"Every step of the way. He'd come home to die."

She'd forgotten the coffee. "You know, I remember the day he was born. I watched him grow up. You know that apple tree out in the back of their house? He fell out of it one time and cracked the bone in his elbow. Claude had their car at work, so I drove Fred to the hospital for an X ray."

Her hand was at her mouth now, and I hardly heard the words. "I was thinking about that today. I was thinking how the last time I took him to the hospital, I could bring him back."

She broke then. Tears streamed down under her glasses, over her hand. She was so tired after all these months, more months than I knew. Aunt Fay strangling on her sobs to keep them back was like the end of everything. I thought the kitchen floor would crack open and swallow us whole.

In a blurry voice she said, "You go on to school."

"Can you get some sleep?"

"I've got to get over to Wilma." She was pulling herself together, trying to. "And I want to clean up Fred's room. It's—I want to make it right for Will. Go on to school. Don't make me tell you again."

I don't remember the science test. Then after school when I was coming down the steps in a crowd, Will was waiting out by the street. He hadn't been in school, but now he was watching for me. And what was I going to say? I'd never had a dad to lose.

"You want to walk over to the park?" he said in his new crackling-deep voice. It was cold, and the park was in the other direction.

"Sure."

It wasn't much of a park. The water tower for the town was in the middle of it, and some picnic tables were dotted around. But I saw why we'd come. Nobody was there. We sat up on a picnic table with our feet on the bench.

"Your aunt Fay wanted me to come find you," he said after a while.

"She'd want you to get out for some air."

"She wanted me to tell you about how my dad died. She said it was my story to tell."

"I know he died in the van," I said, trying to be careful. "You were with him."

"He had AIDS."

My hand grabbed the table because I thought it was

rocking. When I looked at Will, he wasn't looking at anything.

"Shouldn't he have been in a hospital before now? Couldn't they—"

"Not here. Your aunt Fay drove him up to see a doctor at the clinic in"—he named a town up the road on the other side of the river. "She took him up there two or three times in the fall when he could still travel. I went with them once. We couldn't take him to the hospital here. Except last night when he was dying. Word would have gotten around."

Still, I couldn't get this into my head. They'd been hiding Will's dad in their house because he had AIDS.

"They rent," Will said.

"What?"

"Grandma and Grandpa don't own their house. They rent. They couldn't take the chance the landlord would throw us out if he knew."

"So they said your dad was in jail?"

Will's elbows were on his knees, his chin on his balled-up fist. "If you've got somebody in jail, people don't ask."

I guess that made sense. It was one lie instead of many.

The wind came up, swirling black leaves. I wanted to give Will something. I wracked my brain until I thought of what it was.

"My mother was an addict. A druggie. She probably still is."

"My dad was a user too. Not a lot, but when he could get it. It was only a part of him, and I thought it didn't matter."

I felt the anger rising in Will. It blew out of him in one sharp blast. "They had a good time, didn't they? Your mom. My dad. They had a good time, and they didn't care."

"They didn't know," I said. "They never thought it could get them."

We sat there for a long time before he said something I didn't catch. "What?"

"I said he was the best dad in the world. He was fun. See, I never wanted anything from him. Not even the dirt bike. I just wanted him. But for months now I'd wake up every morning, and there'd be less of him there. He couldn't do anything for himself. He couldn't keep himself clean. Your aunt Fay had to—I'm not going to remember that."

I took a chance and said, "Then it's better now that it's over?"

"It's not over," Will said. "It's just started. Now people will know."

He wasn't in school on Friday. At lunch I went upstairs to the library. It was just the end of the second-floor hall with a door. There was no room to browse and not that many books. Ms. Lovett was in there, being librarian over lunchtime. She looked nicer on the days she didn't wear black. I'd been wishing I could look like her when I was older.

"What can I help you find?" Her big eyes looked up from a stack of workbook pages.

"Do you have anything about AIDS?"

She glanced at the shelf. "No, they wouldn't have anything here. Have you tried the public library?"

I panicked. The wind went out of me, and I couldn't breathe. Why was I bringing this up? It was like I was spreading the word. Like I'd betrayed Will. The McKinneys had been so careful, and now I was running my mouth. Why hadn't I gone to the public library in the first place? I didn't go there anymore since Tracy, but so what?

"I'll try there," I said, and I couldn't wait to get away from Ms. Lovett. "It's for science class," I said, but she knew I was lying.

After school I had to go to the rest room, the famous rest room where I popped Rocky Roberts last September. Somebody was smoking in the next stall, but I knew it wasn't Rocky. I hadn't cured him of smoking, but I'd cured him of smoking in here.

When I was at the sink, Brandi Breathwaite came out of that stall. Both the other sinks were free, but she sidled up next to me and pushed her face in my mirror. She had a lot of bounce and big hair. If she wasn't careful, she'd end up a cheerleader. I'll tell you who

Brandi was. She was one of those girls sitting next to Will and me in the auditorium on the first day, the one who put out her hand so I wouldn't sit next to her.

"Hey, Molly," she said, digging in a bag and bringing up the dirtiest hairbrush I ever saw. I knew everybody in school now, at least by name. But I was never ready when anybody knew me.

She leaned forward and grinned into the mirror to scratch a fleck of tobacco off a tooth. "So what have you got to tell me about Will McKinney?"

I was bent over the sink, rinsing soap off my hands, hurrying now.

"You think it's a secret?" she said. "Please." Now she was putting on a lot of red lipstick, brighter than Jungle Red. Her hair and face filled up the mirror.

"I don't know what you're talking about." Was I going to have to pop her one? She was bigger than Rocky.

"Forget about it," she said. "Everybody knows. Will McKinney cut school yesterday, then showed up to meet you afterward. Are you kidding me? Everybody saw."

I went weak in the knees. That's all she meant? She thought Will and I were boyfriend-girlfriend? That was it? I was so relieved I could have kissed her, almost.

"He's cute," she said. "It's like I just noticed. He's cute."

"Yeah, he's pretty cute," I mumbled.

She glanced my way, wondering what he saw in me.

"Of course he's no Nelson Washburn," she said.

Like she could ever get near Nelson Washburn. With that hair and all that paint on her mouth? Please.

"Nelson likes Selena Schmidt," I said, picking out of the air a girl who sat behind me in math. I wasn't good at girl talk, but good enough to fool Brandi.

"You're kidding me," she said.

"Common knowledge."

She had somebody she wanted to tell this to, so she was jamming all her stuff into her bag. But I was out of there before she was.

The relief washed over me all the way home. People weren't going to find out that Will's dad died of AIDS. Even if it got around among the grown-ups, kids at school wouldn't hear about it. They never paid much attention to grown-ups anyway, or what they said. So Will wouldn't have to pay for what had happened to his dad. That's what I thought because that's what I wanted to think.

They buried his dad on Saturday afternoon. It was early March, and the sun came and went. The McKinneys rode in the funeral car behind the hearse. Aunt Fay and I followed in the Dart. We pulled off the gravel and waited for the undertaker's people to lift the casket out.

Then as Will and his grandma were helping Mr. McKinney out of the funeral car, somebody pulled up and parked behind us. A tall man walked past, a long gray overcoat flapping around his legs. "That'll be the preacher," Aunt Fay said. "The mortician arranged for him. He cut it close."

He went up to the McKinneys and tried to shake Mr. McKinney's hand.

"Did you ever go to church?" I asked Aunt Fay. There was a church on every corner in this town.

"I never had the clothes for it," she said, "and I always worked Sundays."

When they started down the slope, helping Mr. McKinney along, Aunt Fay and I got out of the car and followed. The McKinneys owned a cemetery plot on the side of the second hill. It may have been the only thing in the world they owned. We stood in a little knot beside a patch of fake grass where the casket rested. There weren't any flowers. With the outdoors around them, Mrs. McKinney and Aunt Fay looked smaller than they were, hunched in their winter coats. I watched the back of Will's neck. He never flinched or wavered while the preacher spoke words the breeze carried away.

Then it was over, and we were coming back up the slope to the cars. The empty hearse moved away, and the funeral car crept off behind it. But Aunt Fay sat behind the wheel with her hands in her lap. She and Mrs. McKinney wouldn't break down in front of

Claude and Will. But it was just us now, so I didn't know. Her face had been carved out of stone all afternoon.

"There's things they can do now for what Fred had," she said finally. "But he didn't have insurance. And I didn't know enough. I couldn't even keep him comfortable."

She looked away out her side window, out across the tombstones. "If I'm useless," she said, "who am I?"

Chapter

12

.
.
.

Spring came in a hurry here, before I knew it. The wind softened, and I felt the year revolving under my feet. Bare branches began to bud, and I remembered the heavy green shade of the trees, last summer when I'd come.

I'd only catch glimpses of Will—he left early for school—but there was something set hard in his face. The coach put a softball team together, and Will went out for it. He did a lot of work around the McKinneys' house too, spring clean-up. You'd see him up on their porch roof, taking out the storms and putting in the screens. He kept moving.

Aunt Fay said she didn't like Claude's color, and the change of seasons unsettled him, so she was over next door at the McKinneys' as much as before. I could have gone with her now. They'd buried their secret. But I didn't because they were hurting over there, and I shied away from that.

I was a little lost and drifty, so almost every time

Aunt Fay went to Mrs. Voorhees's house, I tagged along. "You ought to learn how to give me a shot," she said, "so I can fire Fay."

Just a joke.

We were over there one day after school. Mrs. Voorhees had some new feel-good medicine she'd talked out of her doctor. She wanted Aunt Fay to be there in case of side effects.

We were late because Aunt Fay had been sitting with Mr. McKinney. When we got to her room, Mrs. Voorhees was on the bed, dressed, holding her head up off the pillow because she'd been to the beauty parlor. It looked like she'd raced up to bed a minute before we got there.

"Where you been?" she said to Aunt Fay, real snappish. She even held up her bedside clock and shook it in the air. "I could have been going into convulsions by now. Fay, I have a notion to dock your pay."

I waited for Aunt Fay to jerk a knot in her tail. But she didn't. She wasn't the same these days, not since Will's dad died. She stood at the end of the bed, gazing at Mrs. Voorhees like she was something in a zoo.

"Well, I went ahead and took that medicine. By now I could be having a conniption . . ." Mrs. Voorhees's whiny voice tailed off.

Still, Aunt Fay just stood there. She didn't even plant a hand on her hip. It was like the game the two of them had always played didn't work anymore.

Mrs. Voorhees couldn't stand the silence. "What's got stuck in your craw anyway, Fay?"

Another long pause, and I felt a squirm up my spine. Then Aunt Fay said, "I've got a lot of responsibilities, Edith, and you're the least of them."

Yes, the game was surely over.

"I've got a responsibility to Wilma McKinney."

Mrs. Voorhees turned over one of her little manicured paws, to brush Wilma McKinney aside. But she didn't dare say anything.

"There's limits to how much Wilma can lose. I couldn't save Fred, but I'm trying to keep Claude going. I couldn't save her son, Edith, so I'm trying to save her man."

Mrs. Voorhees rallied a little. "Well, Fay, you don't have to take my head off. You and Wilma always were too thick to stir."

"And I've got responsibilities to Wilma's grandson too. He's a thirteen-year-old boy, and he's lost his dad, and he don't know how to grieve."

I thought Mrs. Voorhees might be sinking into the bedclothes by now. But she sat straight up and locked eyes with Aunt Fay.

"Don't lecture me about loss, Fay. I've lost my full share. I've lost what you never had, and you know it."

She looked fierce and feisty. I thought she might jump out of the bed. She was wearing shoes.

But Aunt Fay kept on. "And I've got responsibilities to this girl here." She pointed at me, though Mrs.

Voorhees's eyesight wasn't that bad. The air crackled between them. They went on talking with their eyes, but I couldn't hear.

"We've all got responsibilities, Edith," Aunt Fay said. "Even you."

Then she walked across the mirrored room, refusing to limp.

Something had happened, and I didn't know what. Aunt Fay looked back at me and said, "Out."

When we were both at the door, Mrs. Voorhees spoke in a frail voice from the bed. "Are you coming tomorrow, Fay?"

"Yes," Aunt Fay said. "I need the work."

She didn't say a word in the car, and I couldn't think of one. Why couldn't she go back to being the way she'd been, getting sassed by Mrs. Voorhees and sassing her back? Why did things have to keep changing, even here?

When we turned onto Cedar, I saw a car parked in front of our house. No, I didn't think Debbie. Not even in my dreams now. We saw a light in the kitchen when we pulled into the garage. But it could have been anybody.

When we came in, a big man in a sweatshirt with a whistle around his neck was getting up from the chair. I looked twice and saw it was the coach from school. Will was sitting at the table.

"Mrs. Moberly? Coach Allen." He whipped off his

ball cap and looked at Will. "He said to bring him here."

People felt pretty free to wander into other people's kitchens around here, but Coach Allen looked uncomfortable. Will pushed back from the table and hiked up his pant leg. His leg was bandaged from knee to sock. "He was sliding to third and bunged up his leg."

Still, Will didn't say anything. "He didn't want me to bring him to his grandparents," the coach said. "Says you're a nurse."

Aunt Fay was over by Will now. Some blood had soaked through, and the bandages were already unraveling. I read her mind. She thought a man had done the wrapping.

"We took him over to Miss Throckmorton," the coach said. "She fixed him up."

Aunt Fay propped Will's ankle on the edge of the table. Sending me for the scissors, she cut the bandages away, and Will wouldn't wince when the cotton stuck to the blood. A patch of skin was missing, and there were some deeper digs.

"There's still dirt in this wound." She sent me to her supply cupboard and worked over Will's leg, cleaning it with soap and water from an enamel pan. When she sprayed the disinfectant on, he dropped his head and clenched his eyes. I noticed how the sideburns were beginning to grow down the sides of his face.

She worked quick and quiet, bandaging and taping

his leg up into a neat, smooth package. You could have put it in the mail. Will made a move, but she laid a hand on his shoulder.

"That's as neat a piece of work as I ever saw," the coach said. "I'm all thumbs." He stood there, swatting his ball cap against his sweatpants. "You could give Miss Throckmorton a lesson—ma'am," he said, eyeing the back door.

Aunt Fay wasn't stopping him, but he had something to say first. Her eyes narrowed behind the glasses. You didn't beat around the bush with her.

"Why don't you keep him home from school for a few days," the coach said, looking at the floor. "Say a week."

"That's for his grandmother to decide," Aunt Fay said. "But he can go to school on that leg. If you want to keep him on the bench till it clears up, that's your business."

The coach worked a hand around the back of his neck. "Mrs. Moberly, what I'm trying to say is there's going to be trouble here. He's lost some blood. There were some splatters. The other boys are already—"

"Don't that happen when you're playing ball?" she said. "Didn't you ever see that before?"

"Mrs. Moberly, you're making it tough on me."

"Then talk plain," she said. "I do."

The coach heaved a sigh and looked over at me. He wanted me out of the room, but I wasn't going.

"Ma'am, you know how people are. Kids. They

know how his daddy died. They don't want his blood on them."

A silence smoldered in the room. Will stared at the floor.

"They won't get anything from him," Aunt Fay said in a low voice, not wanting to say this. "He's healthy, if it's anybody's business but his own. I had him tested one time when I took his dad to the clinic."

"Then you thought—"

"I didn't think anything," Aunt Fay said, full-voiced again. "But I saw this day coming." She pointed at the coach. "I didn't know what shape it would take, but I saw it coming."

"Well, ma'am—"

"Don't ma'am me," she said. "I'm mad. If the kids at that school are so dumb they think you can get HIV from a splatter of blood out of just anybody, it's up to you to educate them. What's a school for if not to teach?"

She waited for an answer.

"We teach them, but they don't hear," the coach said. "They only listen to each other."

That was true. I felt a little sorry for him, and not just because he'd come up on Aunt Fay's wrong side, on the wrong day. He left then.

Another silence fell on us.

Then Aunt Fay said, "I'm going over to look in on Wilma. You two talk it out. You're the ones who have to go to that school."

Will looked up as she turned to go. "What are you going to tell Grandma?"

"All I know," Aunt Fay said. "You skinned up your leg sliding to third, and I dressed it." The screen door snapped shut behind her.

We sat there, listening to the throb of the motor inside the icebox.

"Miss Throckmorton worked on me too fast to do a good job," Will said at last. "She wanted me out of there. And she wore rubber gloves."

"Maybe they're supposed to."

"Did she wear rubber gloves that time you whipped Rocky Roberts's tail?"

"No. But—"

"You know what it reminded me of? Watching my dad die in the van. The paramedics wore rubber gloves and face masks and these big disposable paper cuffs. They looked like they were on a moon shot. Like as-tronauts. I couldn't see their faces. So it was just me and my dad. Then not even him."

I didn't know what to say. His eyes were hard as rocks.

"Does it hurt?" I said finally.

"You mean my leg?"

I glanced around the kitchen. I ought to be busy doing something. That was the Aunt Fay in me. "She was steamed anyway, before we got home," I said, beating around the bush.

"Why?"

"She and Mrs. Voorhees got into it. Serious this time."

"What about?"

"Seems like it was about me, but I don't know."

We sat there. "Well anyway," I said, "you got a ride home."

"He only brought me home to say I ought to stay home," Will said. "He's trying to keep the lid on. If I'm on the team, he's afraid parents will start complaining."

I saw what he meant, but I wasn't used to him seeming this much older.

"You've got a right to play on the team," I said. I didn't know why anybody would want to play on a team, but it was something to say. And he was a guy.

"Right," he said. "Or I could take the report from the clinic that says I'm clean and post it in the locker room." His voice was all sharp edges. "Like I owe them an explanation."

"How did the guys find out, anyway?"

"Because they don't let you keep a secret in a town like this. The undertaker probably told. And if he didn't, somebody else would."

I waited, not knowing what to say.

"I'm taking myself off the team."

I tried to read his face. "You sure?"

"It's no big deal. Hey, I got carried away. We've been here all year, and I started following the crowd. I forgot who we are."

Strays—

"I haven't got time to play their games. I've got to be as old as I can be. Grandpa calls me Fred now."

After a little bit, I said, "But you liked having lunch over at the team table."

"I'd just as soon have lunch with you," he said, not looking at me.

"Just as soon?"

"Sooner."

I wondered if I'd gotten off easy. My mother just drifted away. "You sure nobody's going to—"

"By next Monday everybody'll be talking about something else."

I hoped so. "When you slid into third base," I said, "who'd you splatter?"

"If I splattered anybody," he said, beginning to smile, "it was Nelson Washburn. And I'd been working up a pretty fair pitching arm too. He didn't like that either."

Now we were both grinning, but his grin was thin.

"Listen, you want to walk to school together tomorrow?" Will said. "That way both of us would know two people."

We did. We even walked all the way there on the same side of the street. When we came up the school steps together, there was Brandi Breathwaite, making big eyes and pointing us out to her girls. She'd pegged us for a twosome ever since that day Will cut school, and Brandi knows it all. Ask her.

In language arts that day Ms. Lovett had written on the blackboard of her portable:

> *By the rude bridge that arched the flood,*
> *Their flag to April's breeze unfurled,*
> *Here once the embattled farmers stood,*
> *And fired the shot heard round the world.*

She read us the whole poem, I guess because it was April. It was the last thing she ever wrote on that blackboard.

And it was true that by next Monday everybody was talking about something else. Will got that right.

Chapter
13
.
.
.

The sirens went off late Sunday night. It was bedtime, but I was still at my table, doing a little homework. I'd kept my Debbie notebook around, and I was
using the blank pages at the back to take notes. It was
warmer than April, and from someplace way off, the
scent of lilacs wafted in the window. Then the sound
of sirens.

First the one in the courthouse tower. Pretty soon
the firetruck's. Then a kind of whispering night breeze
like everybody in town was asking, "Where is it? How
near is it?"

The gate between us and the McKinneys' squeaked.
From down in our yard, Will said, "Molly? They say
it's the junior high."

Sunday night and the school's on fire? I was downstairs in two jumps.

Aunt Fay rose up from the living-room couch. She'd
been dozing, still dressed. "Where is it?"

"Will says it's the school." I was aimed at the front
door, hoping she'd let me go. Her feet hit the floor,

and her head disappeared as she scrabbled around for her shoes. "I haven't missed a fire yet," she said, rounding the couch, grabbing for her car keys. Then she and Will and I were driving the long way around on side streets, closing in on the school.

We followed a glow in the sky until we saw they'd blocked off the street. Aunt Fay swerved to the curb, and we walked from there past people in their pajamas on porches.

We were in a mob when we came to the school. It was still there, black against smoky orange light with bits of burning shingle spiraling up into the night sky. "It could be the new building," Will said, meaning the gym and cafeteria.

It was a couple of portables, Ms. Lovett's and another one, going up like bonfires. The firemen were dragging hoses. A half-moon of people stood as close as they could get with the glow of the fire on their faces. When the water arched up, they made that sound they make for fireworks.

But it was too late, and all I could think was how neat Ms. Lovett had always kept the top of her desk. We stayed until both portables were sizzling piles of embers.

It looked like half the student body of the junior high had turned out, hanging on till the end. Even then, a question was murmuring through the crowd:

"Where's Rocky?"

That was one Monday morning nobody minded going to school. Will and I got there early to look over the ruins. The portables were just bent metal and broken glass and black patches on the grass. But there'd been another fire too. A little one had licked up the far side of the gym, but they'd got that out before it could really take hold. A cop car was pulled up, and they had the back of the gym taped off. They were taking pictures of an empty can that people said had gas or paint thinner in it.

When the bell rang, we milled around like the first day of school while they tried to find us classroom space. Finally we had some language arts on the auditorium stage. Ms. Lovett looked near tears. But you know how it is. Everybody was pretty excited.

Rocky Roberts wasn't in school. Maybe this was just one of his days for not being here. But by lunch people said he'd lit out. By sixth period they said the cops were holding him at a roadblock. If the school day had run any longer, they'd have had Rocky convicted and serving time.

Now that Will's dad was gone, Aunt Fay had taken on a couple of new patients. She came in late that Monday night. If she'd been a minute later, I'd have answered the phone. It rang as she walked in the kitchen door. I was waiting supper for us.

"That's right," I heard her say. Then "I believe she mentioned it." Then "I'd sooner you tell me now, over the phone." I wasn't paying much attention. I was stirring up a can of soup. "Well, all right, I'll come," Aunt Fay said. "No, I'm going to bring her. She knows you folks, and I don't."

She hung up. I stopped stirring.

"A Mrs. Pringle?" she said.

Tracy.

"She's the one who gave me the clothes. Why—"

"I don't know. But it sounds worse than she's letting on. She wants me to go up there. It's cooler tonight. Slip something on and show me the way."

My mind was a blank all the way up the hill. I showed Aunt Fay where to turn and the Pringles' house. A light was on over the door. I'd never expected to be here again.

The front door opened, and it was Mrs. Pringle, almost every hair in place, looking past us as she ushered us inside.

"Yes. Molly, isn't it?" Her eyes swept over me to Aunt Fay. "Very good of you to come. I'd just like you to have a look at my daughter. I'm sure it's not—"

"Where is she?" Aunt Fay said.

She'd be in her bedroom with all the white flounces and framed flowers. When Mrs. Pringle saw I was following them up the carpeted stairs, she turned. "You may wait downstairs."

"No," Aunt Fay said. "She can come."

Mrs. Pringle caught her breath but wouldn't take

the time to argue. I wasn't sure where I wanted to be. I hadn't seen this house at night. It was all shadows. And I didn't go farther than the door of Tracy's room. It was dim, with one light on beside the canopied bed. Someone—Tracy was lying on top of the covers. I just glimpsed. She didn't seem to have a lot of clothes on. All I could think of was how many clothes she had and how few she was wearing.

Aunt Fay was around on the far side of the bed, and Mrs. Pringle was beside her, hovering. Then Aunt Fay put up her hands and stepped back. It wasn't like her. It wasn't a move she made. "What in the world has happened to this child?"

"It was—we were burning some trash," Mrs. Pringle said.

Tracy was awake. I saw her head move, but Aunt Fay turned on Mrs. Pringle. "Call an ambulance."

"Surely you can do some—"

"Do it or I will." Aunt Fay's finger was in Mrs. Pringle's face. "Where's the phone?"

It wasn't in this room. Tracy wasn't allowed to have a phone.

"Who's your doctor?"

"I didn't want to bother—"

"Get an ambulance first. This child is seriously burned. Go now."

I stood aside when Mrs. Pringle went out the door. Then Aunt Fay said from across the room, "Molly, go downstairs and wait in the living room."

I didn't go. I didn't want to be that far from Aunt Fay. It was babyish, but I was scared. I didn't want to sit down there in that big perfect living room by myself. The whole house was too empty. It dawned on me that Tracy didn't have a dad. It was one thing we had in common, though she'd never mentioned it.

Mrs. Pringle came out of another room and went back to Tracy's. Her face was like a mask. I could hear some of what she and Aunt Fay said. It was like listening at the door in a dream.

"This child's arm is burned to the shoulder. And the side of her face." There was a snap in every word Aunt Fay spoke.

"Will she be disfigured?"

"That's the least of your worries. When did this happen?"

". . . This afternoon. We were—"

"I don't think so. You've lost a lot of time here. I don't know what you were thinking about. Did you call your doctor to meet—"

"No. It was my decision not to." Mrs. Pringle's voice sounded nearly like herself again.

Then in the distance, the sound of a siren.

"I told them no siren," Mrs. Pringle said, her voice rising. "And you're no help to me. I didn't know where to turn. You were the only person I could think of. I thought you'd help me."

I went downstairs to let in the paramedics when they got there. It seemed an age. But then the siren got louder and louder. I opened the door and pointed them upstairs. Then I stood in the yard because I didn't want to be in the house.

They carried Tracy out past me. But I didn't look at her. I thought she wouldn't want me to. Aunt Fay came out of the house and walked straight to the Dart. Mrs. Pringle came last, turning back to lock the door.

We sat in the car while Aunt Fay watched her rearview mirror, flashing blue. We were waiting for the van to pull out of the drive behind us.

"Are we going to the hospital with them?" I asked her.

"No. I got the name of their doctor out of her. I'll tell him she called me in, but I wash my hands of this. He'll have to deal with the situation as he sees fit."

Did she mean Tracy's burns?

The van pulled out behind us, and we were there in the dark. "I'm sick to death of secrets," Aunt Fay said.

Rocky Roberts swaggered into school Tuesday morning. He wasn't even late. The crowds parted for him, but that was nothing new. Same old Rocky. He hadn't grown an inch all year. Will said maybe his grandma Marlene mopping and waxing the floor with him had stunted his growth. But Rocky still knew how to look dangerous. He had a cigarette parked over one ear, and that reminded people of matches. And matches reminded them of fire.

The story made the Tuesday newspaper, with a picture on the front page of soot on the gym wall:

MINOR DAMAGE IN MYSTERY FIRE THAT CONSUMED TWO PORTABLE UNITS
ARSON SUSPECTED

By Wednesday Nelson Washburn thought student government ought to go in a body to Mr. Russell to find out why Rocky was still walking around free. Nelson campaigned about this in the lunchroom. He even leaned over me to talk it up with Will.

Until Will said, "Not too close, Washburn. I might bleed on you."

The murmuring and muttering went on all week. Finally one of the girls in Brandi Breathwaite's bunch seemed to recall seeing Rocky on Sunday night, running from tree to tree with a can of gas in his hand. We watched Rocky like a hawk, but do you know something? I don't think he noticed.

I watched him with the rest. I hadn't paid that much attention to him all year because he never looked me in the eye. But now I watched him, though not for the same reason the others did. Did whipping his tail last September build something between us? I don't think so, but Rocky was a stray like me. He never told his history because nobody ever asked. There was this space around him too.

Of course Brandi Breathwaite was another stray. Hadn't she been in the auditorium with us that first day? But she moved in a pack of other girls, so it looked like she'd come from here. By now she probably thought she had. It was funny how I could relate better to rotten old Rocky than to her.

But then, I knew Rocky hadn't tried to burn down the school.

How much did I know that night when I hung at the edge of Tracy's room? Seemed like I never could just know something—it had to creep up on me. But the sheriff called Aunt Fay down to the courthouse to give a statement about going to the Pringles' house. And she got the story from him and came home to tell me. It was Tracy who'd set the fires.

But I had to see it for myself, in my mind. I had to picture Tracy going up to her room that Sunday night. I supposed she had an early bedtime. I saw her in her bed wearing jeans—no, gray-flannel slacks—and a sweater under her nightgown. I tried to be Tracy—staying awake till the house got even quieter and her mother was asleep. Then I felt her throw back the covers, and I watched her carrying her shoes down the carpeted stairs and out the back door that she'd left open a little.

I saw Tracy dodge in the dark down to the garage,

where she'd left a can full of something that would make a fire burn hot. Paint thinner, because their house looked freshly painted. I felt the lump of the matchbook in her pocket.

Then, stranger still, she disappeared across the town—Tracy, whose mother never let her walk anywhere. But Tracy knew the way, down the hill and along the side streets, not noticing the scent of the lilacs. She'd learned the way to school before she had to go there, just like I'd done last summer. And maybe she moved from tree to tree.

She went around behind school where nobody would see her from the street. Maybe she thought the portables would burn faster. They did, too fast, so she hurried, panicked by the light. She slopped what was left in the can against the gym wall and touched another match. But this one touched her. I made myself feel that flame hit the paint thinner on her hand and coil like a snake up her sweater. Then she was running, which was just the wrong thing to do. But she was running from the light, running for home and her mother.

Aunt Fay didn't say I couldn't tell anybody. But I didn't say a word, not even to Will. I guess I wasn't as sick to death of secrets as Aunt Fay was. Maybe it was like that moment when they'd carried Tracy past me on the stretcher and I hadn't looked at her because I'd thought she wouldn't want me to.

If I told, it would just sound like another rumor. Nobody knew Tracy Pringle. It'd be a lot more interesting if it was somebody everybody knew. Rocky, for instance. Besides, I thought it would all come out in the paper. It didn't, and I asked Aunt Fay why.

"They're keeping it quiet," she said. "The girl's underage, and her mama's brought in a lawyer from out of town. They wanted the girl put on the psychiatric ward for observation. But her mama wouldn't hear of it. If you ask me, it's her who's a psycho. Letting that child lie in bed with those burns, just to keep the world from knowing."

Or for fear the world would take Tracy away from her.

"They're going to let her go home."

Back where she started.

"Do you have any idea why she'd try to burn down the school?" Aunt Fay said, watching me. "She didn't even go there."

I didn't know why, but I was the only one who knew Tracy. I had to try to understand.

I decided she'd wanted to burn down the school because she didn't go there. All the rest of us were there every day. But she only dressed in the kind of school clothes nobody really wore and went to school at the dining-room table with her mother. She was the one with the most space around her of us all, and she wasn't even a stray.

I guess the loneliness crept up on her. She thought

we all had each other. She thought school was a party, with boys. Maybe she even envied me. Then one day she was fourteen years old, and everybody else had someplace to be. And she wanted to burn it down.

Or maybe she just wanted to do something so terrible, they'd take her a long way away from her mother, farther from her mother than I was from mine.

"I don't know why," I said to Aunt Fay, because you can't really see inside somebody else's heart, even in a town like this where sooner or later every secret comes to light.

Knowing that Tracy set the fires was a lot to keep from telling. I made a deal with myself to tell Will later, when we were older. Eighth grade, maybe. Or the year after that, high school. That was looking ahead, and I wasn't used to looking ahead. But I was beginning to.

Chapter
14
.
.
.

The letter came during the last week of the semester. It was already too summery for school, but the end was in sight. I came home one afternoon, and Aunt Fay was at the kitchen table. She never just sat, so she was waiting for me, and the letter was in her hand. I couldn't read her face, but I read the envelope. It was from the Division of Family and Youth Services.

It slowed me down. I worked my way over to the other chair, and she nodded me into it.

"You remember that woman who brought you here?"

The social worker. Yes, I remembered. I felt the floor shift under me like the year was beginning to come full circle, and we'd be back where we began, or somewhere farther back than that.

"This letter's from the office that sent her. Do you want to read it?" She turned the letter on the table. It was two pages.

"Tell me," I said.

"It's about your mother. About Debbie."

"Is she dead?"

The question came from some deep place. I didn't see it coming.

"Oh, Molly, no. She's not dead." Aunt Fay smacked the table with the flat of her hand. "What's wrong with me? Why didn't I know you might think that?"

"It's all right," I said. "Just tell me."

"They got her for selling dope. 'Controlled substance,' they call it. They've got her in a lockup."

I didn't ask where. I just saw her in a cell someplace, and I thought she was as safe there as Debbie could be. I saw her in a cell, but I couldn't remember her face.

"She's fighting it," Aunt Fay said.

I saw Debbie reach up and grab hold of the bars on the windows, trying to shake them loose.

"She says she can't be sentenced and put away because she's a mother. Because of you."

Did she want me back to keep her out of jail? Is that all she wanted me for?

"Could I keep her out of jail?"

"Not in a million years. But she's playing games with the system. She's got to waive her rights to you when she's sentenced, and she says she won't do it. Don't that sound like her? Making trouble to keep from taking her medicine?"

Maybe it sounded like her. Had I let myself forget too much about her?

"They'll declare her an unfit mother, and she'll serve

her time. And that'll be that." Aunt Fay's voice trailed off.

"But what?" I said, studying her.

"But it's brought your name up on the computer or whatever. They should have been checking on you right along. Your well-being. They ought to have been sending a caseworker down regular."

"Why didn't they?"

"Because they're the government," she said. "But now somebody's going to come down and look us over."

"Soon?"

"One of these days. They're going to set up an appointment." She'd pushed back from the chair and propped her ankle on her knee. She was thinking, but I didn't know what.

"Could they take me away and put me in foster care?"

"Over my dead body!" But she clamped a hand over her mouth at the thought. "It's given me an idea, though." She tapped the letter with that finger she pointed at people. "It's given me the push I need."

I could read her mind now, a little. She was up to something. "Tonight me and you are going up the hill and pay a call on Edith Voorhees. I'll phone ahead so she'll be sure to be in bed."

That didn't sound like anything new, but then she said, "Wear your worst clothes."

Did I hear that right?

"That sweatshirt that ran in the wash? Wear that. You can wear them jeans you've got on. Your knees are coming through."

"That's the way they wear them at school."

"But Edith won't know it."

Then Aunt Fay winked at me. I'd never seen her do that. I thought she had something in her eye.

We sat with the summer afternoon sliding in across the kitchen table, and I had a peculiar thought. Would I look back on this moment as the last of something, or the start? It was one of those thoughts that's here and gone again.

I looked down and pointed. "You've lost your ankle bracelet."

"No, I took it off." She pursed up her lips like it didn't matter. "Moberly give it to me before we were married. You know, when men give you presents. I said I'd never take it off, and I never did while he was alive. But it was beginning to cut off the circulation in my foot. Gold shrinks, you know."

"Aunt Fay, gold don't shrink."

"Gold doesn't shrink," she said. "Watch your grammar."

There was still some purple in the sky when we drove up the hill to Park Place and swung into Mrs. Voorhees's drive. I expected Aunt Fay to heave herself out of the Dart and tramp up to the front door as usual. But I noticed she hadn't brought her black nurse's bag. It was such a part of her, I never noticed until it wasn't there. She sat a minute, thumping the steering wheel with her knuckles.

Finally she said, "Well, here goes nothin'."

She elbowed the door open, and we went on in and up the curving stairs and into Mrs. Voorhees's room.

She was sitting on top of her bed in one of the long dresses she called "hostess gowns." Shoes too. Little gold sandals with their high heels digging into the bedspread. She was all painted up and glittering.

"Where's your bag?" she said sharpish to Aunt Fay. "I need—"

"This is a social call," Aunt Fay said, "and you don't need a thing."

Only a small spark arced between them, so I thought they were back to normal, sassing each other. Mrs. Voorhees's eyes skated over me.

Then Aunt Fay did something she'd never done before. She sat down on the bed, right beside Mrs. Voorhees's knees.

"Well, make yourself at home," Mrs. Voorhees said. "Fay, what's come over you this time?"

"I'll get right to the point, Edith. I know how you like to have everything out in the open."

"Well, I—"

"I've had a letter today." Aunt Fay reached down

into the front of her top and pulled out the envelope. "Here." She held it out. "You better read it for yourself."

"Well, I—"

"Oh, I forgot," Aunt Fay said. "You're blind as a bat without your glasses."

Mrs. Voorhees bristled.

"It's from the Division of Family and Youth Services."

I stood beside the bed, watching something happen.

"As you can imagine, it's about Molly. And her mother."

Mrs. Voorhees pulled back against the pillows. "What does it say?" she said in no more than a whisper.

"Do you want to hear it all?" Aunt Fay flipped the flap on the envelope.

"Just sum it up."

"They've got Debbie on a drug charge. She's going up for a long stretch on this one. But then she was dealing drugs when she was in high school, wasn't she? Way back then."

"I don't know," Mrs. Voorhees whispered. She looked away from both of us. You could only see the tight curls on the back of her head, flattened by the pillow. She'd been to the beauty parlor today. "Why do I have to hear this?" she said.

"For one thing," Aunt Fay said, "I don't know but what they're going to take Molly away from me. They're sending somebody down here from the state."

I opened my mouth, but she looked up at me, and I closed it again.

Mrs. Voorhees's little red-tipped hands were clamped in her lap. "I don't know why they'd do a thing like that," she said, still looking away.

"I can give you three reasons, Edith. I'm about half lame. My house is coming down around my ears. And I'm not blood kin to her."

Mrs. Voorhees unclenched her hands and put one up, like she wanted to push Aunt Fay away.

"You wouldn't let them take her. You'd run them off the place with a shotgun," she said, still talking to the far side of the room. "You and that girl have got too thick to stir. Why are you telling me all this? You know I'm not a well woman. What's this about, Fay?"

"It's about time, Edith."

I looked across the room and saw us, dim, in the mirrors on the closet doors. The three of us—me in my sweatshirt that had run in the wash, between these two old ladies.

Then Aunt Fay spoke in a voice she'd never used. "I'll be everything to this girl I can be for as long as they let me. But she's got more coming to her, for all she never had."

"If it's money—"

"It's not money, Edith. Money won't buy it."

Mrs. Voorhees's hand came up to her shoulder to touch the sunburst pin, which might have been diamonds.

Aunt Fay put out her hand to me, and maybe Mrs. Voorhees saw in the mirrors across the room. I'd never held Aunt Fay's hand, and she didn't touch you for nothing.

"Do you want Molly and me to go now?"

"What for?" Mrs. Voorhees said, aside. "You just got here. What are you saying, Fay? That you won't be back?"

"Oh, I'll be back," Aunt Fay said. "I work for you."

"Just you, is that it?"

"Just me," Aunt Fay said.

Mrs. Voorhees's head began to turn, quivering a little. She looked up at me as if I'd just appeared there, and she blinked.

"Look at the state of that sweatshirt," she said. "You ought to cut it up for rags."

"Shall I skin it off?" I said.

"Not if you don't have a bra on underneath." She turned on Aunt Fay. "Has it come to your attention that this girl is growing up and filling out? She needs undergarments. I have to say it, Fay. I don't think you have the first idea of how to bring up a girl."

"And what do you know about it?"

The air between them went dead. Both their profiles were carved in stone. Then Mrs. Voorhees's hand moved up to her mouth, and her eyes started with tears. The big eyelashes she painted on her lids blurred like they'd run in the wash.

"I had a little girl once!" she cried out, and her eyes overflowed.

Aunt Fay still held me there with them. But she reached over to touch Mrs. Voorhees too. "I know, Edith."

Mrs. Voorhees's hands slid down her face, and she looked up at me. "I had a little girl once."

All by itself my hand reached into the neck of my sweatshirt, and I pulled up the gold chain with the baby ring on it.

"That's right," she said, and all her makeup was washing down her face. "That was hers."

She brought up another sob and reached around in her pocket for a handkerchief.

"Tell her who you are, Edith," Aunt Fay said.

"I'm your grandmother," she said, still looking around for her handkerchief.

The world came and went. I felt dizzy, but Aunt Fay still had me in hand.

"How can you be?" I said. She was Mrs. Voorhees. She was this old lady we went to see in a big house at the top of the hill.

"She married Moberly's brother. Her and me were

married to brothers at one time. He was one of her husbands."

"My second," Mrs. Voorhees said behind the handkerchief. "I only had three."

"Tell it, Edith."

"And we had a little girl, and we named her Debbie."

It got dark then, real quick. I didn't know where I was. When I could find some words, I said to Aunt Fay, "Why didn't you tell me?"

"It wasn't my story to tell. Did I tell you Will McKinney's story? And I didn't tell you Edith's. I was waiting for her to remember."

"Remember?" Mrs. Voorhees balled up the handkerchief. "What do you mean, *remember*, Fay? I had a daughter, and I lost her. She slipped through my fingers. I tried to forget, and I couldn't."

"I was waiting for you to remember what you owe your granddaughter," Aunt Fay said. "I been waiting all year. I'm wore out waiting."

Mrs. Voorhees wanted to look away again. She was wet down her front and dabbed at it with the handkerchief.

"I'm afraid of her," she said in a frail voice.

Of me? How could she be afraid of me?

"Afraid you'll lose her too?" Aunt Fay said in her new voice.

Mrs. Voorhees nodded.

But I couldn't think. She was still Mrs. Voorhees.

She swept the lace handkerchief aside and arranged her hands in her lap. She could use a manicure. I ought to give her a—

"Well, there'll have to be some changes made," she said, sharpish again. "For one thing, Fay, we can't let this girl go around looking like she's run off from the poor farm. We've got to get her some decent clothes. You'd think that stuff she wears came from Marshalls. Honestly."

"Well, whatever you think best, Edith." Aunt Fay climbed to her feet. We were still holding hands, and she gave mine a bone-crusher squeeze. "We'll be back tomorrow," she told Mrs. Voorhees, "because, girl, you've got a shot coming."

We were at the door before Mrs. Voorhees called out from the bed, "And you tell those government people to get off your case. This girl has got a grandmother, and she's not a person they want to trifle with. You got that, Fay?"

"I got it," Aunt Fay said. "They could hear you downtown." Then we left.

Out in the dark car Aunt Fay sat slumped at the wheel, wore out. I sat beside her, feeling the baby's ring in the hollow of my throat. Once, Mrs. Voorhees had said she'd lost what Aunt Fay'd never had. She meant Debbie. The lightning bugs were out that night, and they were like my thoughts.

"Do I have a grandpa too? Is her Moberly husband around somewhere?"

"Oh no, he's out in the cemetery pushing up daisies," Aunt Fay said. "He fell off the grain elevator. Then she married Voorhees and feathered her nest."

So Debbie had only told me half a lie. She always said she was an orphan. That's why I thought she'd had me sent to Aunt Fay. I didn't know she'd just wanted to hurt her mother more. I'd thought Aunt Fay was the nearest thing to kin I had. I still thought it.

"Do I have to go live with her?"

"She can't have you. You live with me. But I took you there on that day last fall when I knew Debbie wasn't coming back. I owed you and Edith that. It was all I could do."

I remembered the day, and Aunt Fay saying she didn't have time to take on another patient. She didn't have the time because she was nursing Will's dad. I remembered the first time we drove up to Park Place, and I'd expected Mrs. Voorhees's house to be a ruined castle with lightning rods.

"She's your grandmother, though it was like pulling teeth to get her to own up. And you're her granddaughter. She lives for the sight of you. Didn't you see?"

We sat in the dark. That was when the tears came, jumping out of my eyes and streaming down my face.

I didn't know that anybody had ever lived for the sight of me.

"But don't look to inherit her money," Aunt Fay said. She knew I was crying. "Edith's going to take it with her when she goes. And when she gets there, it'll all get burned up."

I wiped my wet face with my terrible sweatshirt sleeve and stared at her.

"Just a joke," she said. "And no more secrets. That was the last of them." She kicked the Dart into life and jerked into reverse, and we went home.

Chapter

15

.
.
.

I've lived in this town for a year, and today I'm up in the apple tree in our backyard. It's leafy August, and over there across the McKinneys' fence Will is up in their tree. Mr. McKinney is out on their back porch, in the shade. Mrs. McKinney has put his chair where Will can watch Claude. And Claude can watch Fred because Will is Fred to him now, and always will be.

We've been up our trees fighting the tent caterpillars. A plague of them has swept through town, and they've built these sticky tents full of their squirming babies all over the branches. The fork I sat in last summer is webbed with them.

Will and I have gone up our trees with bug spray and sticks, trying to get rid of them before they eat up all the foliage. I'm halfway to fourteen now, so I'm beginning not to like bugs or getting stuff on my hands. And the caterpillar tents are disgusting—sticky and webby and weird. "Like science fiction," Will says. "Like the Pod People."

A couple more weeks and we'll be in eighth grade.

Something's happened to summer. It melted away before we knew. The social worker they sent to check on me and Aunt Fay has come and gone.

She seemed satisfied with the way we were living, but Aunt Fay didn't let her off easy. We all three went up the hill to pay a call on Mrs.—my grandmother. And she put on a real show for us. She was dressed in her best and downstairs without her cane. Her hands were heavy with diamonds, and the sunburst pin glared from her shoulder. She was high and mighty and talked down her nose to the social worker, who couldn't wait to get away from her.

"And don't put me through anything like that again," Grandmother Edith told Aunt Fay afterward. "You know I'm not a well woman."

As the social worker was leaving, I gave her my notebook. The one with the Debbie pictures on all the pages except for the blank ones at the end where I'd done homework notes. I'd saved it, though the pictures I'd drawn weren't that good. Ms. Lovett was just being nice. But I wanted Debbie to have it if they could get it to her. I wanted her to have the Debbie I carried with me as long as I could.

I loved my mother, and she loved me. She loved me like a rag doll you drag around and then leave out in the rain. I still love her, but I live here.

Will and I have done about all we can do in the war against the tent caterpillars. Now we're taking a breather, up here where you can get some air. We're just sitting. But then in a strange, reedy voice from last year, Will says, "Want to hear a song? I know most of 'Achy, Breaky Heart.' Want to hear it?"

And I think, Why not?